Long Lost Christmas

Long Lost Christmas

A Sweetheart, Montana Romance

Joan Kilby

TULE
PUBLISHING

Chapter One

Wednesday, December 11. Fallbrook, California.

"I FOUND THE decorations." Hayley Stevens carried the box into the living room where her mom, Joyce, was seated on the sofa writing Christmas cards. A cinnamon-scented candle perfumed the air and carols played softly in the background. The rich smells of baking shortbread wafted through from the kitchen.

Hayley set down the box and stepped back to eye the tree critically. "Does it look off-center?"

"It's perfect," Joyce said, glancing up. "I wonder where Brad is? He said he wanted to help decorate the tree."

"I'll give him a call." Hayley pulled out her phone and punched in her brother's number. Between their various work commitments, she hadn't seen him in several months and was looking forward to catching up and having some relaxing family time.

"Yo, sis," Brad said when he picked up. "I tried to call Mom a while ago, but it went straight to voice mail. Do you know if she's home?"

"Yes, she is. I'm here, too, and just about to start the tree," Hayley said. "How long are you going to be?"

"Sorry, I can't make it after all." He spoke loudly, above background noise of people and loudspeakers.

"Oh, no. Why not?" Hayley said. Whatever his reply, it was drowned out by what sounded like a jet taking off. "Where are you?"

"LAX. My plane leaves for the Philippines in half an hour."

"But you said you would be here for Christmas this year." She made a dismayed face at her mother. Brad was a logistics officer, who was the onsite coordinator of aid supplies for Doctors Without Borders, and he often went overseas for weeks. "Will you be back in time?"

"I doubt it. A massive typhoon just slammed into the eastern end of the archipelago," Brad said.

"When did you find this out?" Hayley said. "You could have let us know you were going away. We could have had a quick get-together before you went."

"I had literally twenty-four hours' notice," he said. "Can you put Mom on? We'll be boarding soon."

"Right, I understand." Hayley tried to channel peace and goodwill, but as well as feeling disappointed, she was a little ticked off. Her brother had worked the last two Christmases and was due to have this holiday off. He'd *promised*. It was especially important because this was the first Christmas after their father, Stan, had passed. She wanted both her and Brad to be here to make this holiday as happy as possible for their mom. But, as always, if he was needed, Brad put his hand up to help. She loved him for it; she just hated that she and her mother always seemed to come last. "Okay, stay on the phone. I want to talk to you again quickly after Mom."

She handed her phone to her mother. While her brother repeated his story, Hayley turned on CNN and put the sound down low. Images of the devastation on the tiny islands played on a loop while reporters cataloged the damage so far. She felt sick for all those affected and appalled that her brother was heading straight into the disaster zone.

"I hope Brad will be okay," Joyce said, putting the phone on the coffee table next to her address book.

"Did he hang up already?" Hayley asked. "I wanted to wish him merry Christmas."

"He said they'd started boarding, but you know what those lines are like," her mother said. "Call him back."

"Never mind." Hayley knew how focused Brad was on his job. In his mind, he was gone before the plane left the runway.

She would miss him. Christmas was one of the few times a year they were able to spend time together. Marathon board games and late-night chats about what was going on in their busy lives helped fill the gap over the long months when they rarely saw each other. Now she and her mom had to deal with, not only the loss of her father, but Brad's absence.

Joyce seemed to be thinking along similar lines. "I'm glad you're here, at least."

"I am too." Hayley gave her mom a tender smile. Sadness welled in her then. Brad would come home, but her father wouldn't. This first Christmas without her dad was going to be hard for her too.

She flicked off the TV and reached into the decorations box for the jumbled string of lights. She got them untangled and wound around the tree and then proceeded to carefully hang her favorite glittering balls. It was only two weeks until Christmas. Her mom was late with everything this year—the tree, the cards, the baking. Joyce hadn't wanted to bother at all, claiming it didn't feel like Christmas without her Stan. Hayley had insisted on all their usual beloved rituals. They needed some feel-good moments in a big way.

"I hear we're going to finally get some rain," Hayley commented to change the subject. "We sure need it." On the surrounding hills, browned grass and blackened scrub bore evidence of recent wildfires.

"Wouldn't it be nice to have a white Christmas?" Joyce said wistfully. She licked the flap of the envelope, sealed it, and added it to the growing stack of cards.

"Uh, Mom, we live in Southern California," Hayley said carefully.

"I know that, silly," Joyce said, waving a hand. She got a dreamy far-off look on her face. "I miss having seasons. When I was a girl in Spokane, we would go tobogganing or skiing at this time of year. Sometimes I think it would be nice to move north again."

"How far north?" Living in San Diego, Hayley was only sixty miles or so away from her mom's small town of Fallbrook. If Joyce were to move out of state she wouldn't see her as frequently.

"Oh, don't listen to me. It's just a pipe dream." Joyce selected another card and began to write.

Hayley went back to hanging ornaments. As an interior decorator, she cringed at some of the homemade decorations she and Brad had made as kids, but her mom always said the tree wasn't complete without them. She glanced indulgently at her mother's smoothly coiffed ash-blonde head bent over another card. She was so sentimental.

"I'm writing a card for Brad," Joyce said. "Do you want to sign it? We can make him a care package of some of my home-baked Christmas goodies and the shortbread you're making."

"He would appreciate that." Hayley put down the tinsel and sat next to Joyce on the sofa to sign the card. "Hardly anybody sends real cards anymore. You could save a lot of time and money by sending e-cards."

"I like the personal touch," Joyce said, pasting a stamp on the addressed envelope. "It's nice to receive a handwritten card. It shows your friends and family that you care and are willing to take the time to let them know you're thinking of them."

"Not everyone has the time, but you're right." Hayley had to admire her mother for writing a personal note in each and every one of the dozens of cards she sent. She hesitated, then broached what she knew to be a touchy subject. "Are you sending one to your brother?"

"I don't know where he lives." Joyce spoke lightly, but mention of her brother deepened the fine lines around her eyes and mouth. "I haven't heard from Gordon in over forty years. He hasn't bothered to keep in touch or inform me where he's living."

Hayley put an arm around her mother's shoulder. Joyce's cool, flippant tone didn't fool her; her mom felt the absence of her brother deeply. "I never understood how you could become estranged from your only sibling. Growing up in foster care, you were all each other had." She thought of Brad and shivered to think how easily an estrangement could happen when people didn't stay in touch.

"I don't get it, either," Joyce said. "We used to be so close. When our parents died in the car crash, I was three and Gordie was ten. Even though he was so much older, he always looked out for me. I idolized him."

Kind of like her and Brad, Hayley thought. As a kid, she'd followed him everywhere, eager to do whatever he did, just to be with him.

"As soon as Gordie graduated from high school, he left home to travel and look for work." Joyce's voice wobbled. "It came out of the blue. I had no idea he was going away. The morning he left, I begged him to stay, or to take me with him. He tried to comfort me, but I was hysterical with grief and rage. In the end, he got on that bus, anyway. I felt so abandoned. It was worse even than losing my mother and father."

"You would have been only eleven," Hayley reminded her. "You were still in school. How could he take you?"

"I know." Joyce sighed. "In hindsight I understand, but a child doesn't see all the ramifications, she only feels the loss."

"Did he call or write?" Hayley asked.

"He sent the occasional postcard—always from different, far-away places—but that was almost worse." Joyce looked down at her hands. "Hearing from him reminded me of what I'd lost."

"Postcards aren't much. He could have made more of an effort to stay in touch," Hayley said. "You were his little sister." Maybe Gordon wasn't such a nice person as her mom made out. Or was he just thoughtless? Like the way Brad had neglected to speak to her again before he hung up.

A faint ding sounded from the oven timer.

"The cookies are done. I'll get us some coffee to go with them." Hayley went to the kitchen and pulled the pan of shortbread out, put half-a-dozen pieces on a plate, and poured fresh coffee, adding a dash of cinnamon.

"Here we go," she said, placing a tray on the coffee table. "When was the last time you heard from Gordon?"

Joyce poured cream into her cup. "Ten or twelve years

after he left home, he wrote a letter from Montana. It was only a few lines to say he was working in construction and that he was married with a baby on the way."

"Did you reply?" Hayley asked.

"Not right away," Joyce admitted. "I was married by then. Your brother was a hyperactive two-year-old, and you were a newborn. Your father was away a lot for work, and I was a frazzled young mother. Then I went back to work too. Life was a blur. You'll find out one day." She cast Hayley a wistful glance. "If you ever decide to settle down."

"Mom, don't start," Hayley said mildly. This was an old skirmish, but she knew her mother was proud of her for starting her own interior design business. One day she hoped to marry and have a family, but at the moment that wasn't on the horizon. "When I do settle down and have babies, you'll be an awesome grandmother. In the meantime, tell me more about Gordon."

"I have a photo." Joyce rose and went to the wall unit, bringing out an old album. Leafing through the pages, she found a strip of four small photos from a photo booth of her and her brother, goofing around in different poses. "This was taken a few weeks before he went away."

Hayley studied the photos with a smile. Her mom had a blonde ponytail and a silly grin. Gordon had windblown light brown hair, laughing eyes, and a wide smile. About eighteen years old, he had pleasant, even features. "You're cute! Uncle Gordon is handsome." She paused. "Can I have one of these?"

"Of course." Joyce took a pair of small scissors and cut the strip in half, handing two photos to Hayley. A pensive smile of reminiscence played about her face as she looked down at the photos left in her hand. "About ten months after I got Gordon's letter, I finally wrote back. Pages and pages, telling him everything that had happened to me since he'd left home. About you and your brother and your dad and our home." Her voice broke, and she paused to steady herself. "I told him how much I loved him and that I wanted to see him again…"

"And?" Hayley prompted gently.

"I never heard from him again." Joyce slipped the photos back inside the album. "I was devastated."

"Maybe your letter never reached him," Hayley said. "Maybe he moved."

"Or maybe he decided he didn't need his overemotional little sister in his life after all," Joyce said.

"You're not overemotional. You're loving and kind." Hayley leaned over to hug her mother again. "You've moved yourself quite a bit over the years. Didn't you ever try to find him?"

"Once I went to the state library and looked for him in phone books from Montana, but I couldn't find his name anywhere," Joyce said. "That was years ago, in the days before the internet."

Hayley feigned surprise. "You mean there was a time before the internet?"

"I know, I'm still living in the prehistoric era," Joyce replied dryly. "I like it here."

"He's probably on Facebook," Hayley said.

"Not everyone is on social media," Joyce said. "I'd rather meet my friends in person."

Hayley was long used to her mom's rants against constant connectedness, but this was Joyce's only brother. There had to be some deeper reason that stopped her mother from looking harder for Gordon. Childhood feelings of loss and rejection must be difficult to overcome, she concluded.

"I don't even know if he's alive, much less if he's still living in Montana," Joyce went on. "Anyway, whatever went wrong between us, too much time has passed. It's too late to patch things up now."

"It's never too late." Hayley picked up a Christmas card depicting a snow-covered cabin with a candle glowing in the window. She handed it to her mom along with a pen. "Write to him. I'll track down an address and mail it when I mail the others, along with Brad's parcel." She cut off one of the photos of brother and sister. "Put that inside to remind him of your childhood together."

"I don't know…" Joyce lifted her troubled gaze to meet Hayley's. "Gordon meant so much to me as a child. If he doesn't reply, it would be like losing him all over again."

"You'll never know if you don't try," Hayley said, pressing the pen into her mom's hand. "Go on. It's Christmas. If there's ever going to be a time to reconnect with your brother, it's now. You don't want to get old and then have regrets."

"Well, thank you for not saying I'm old now," Joyce replied jokingly, but she took the card and pen. "Don't look over my shoulder!" she added when Hayley sat there expectantly.

"All right, all right." Hayley rose and went back to decorating the tree.

When she glanced back at her mother, Joyce had a real smile on her face as she wrote in her graceful slanting script. Her mom was right, the personal touch meant so much more.

She was about to place the angel on the top of the tree when an idea struck her. Instead of mailing the card, she would deliver it to her uncle in person. Whatever had caused the long-ago rift, surely, he would feel the passage of time and want to reconnect with his sister. Her mom would be surprised and thrilled to get a phone call. Hayley glanced over at her mother, still writing away. She wouldn't say anything about her plan now, in case she couldn't find Gordon, or worse, in case Joyce was right and he wasn't interested in renewing his relationship with his sister.

"Oh, by the way, Mom." Hayley strived to sound casual.

"Yes, dear," Joyce said absently.

"I, uh, forgot to tell you…I'm going away for a few days next week."

Joyce glanced up, frowning. "But Christmas is two weeks away. Can't it wait until the new year?"

"I'll be back in time, don't worry," Hayley assured her. "It's just that something has come up. I need to go now."

"For a client?"

"No," Hayley said slowly. "It's a thing I'm doing on spec. But it's important. I can't let this opportunity go by. I don't know when I'll have another chance."

"Lydia is coming to stay for a few days next week on her way to see her daughter in Flagstaff," Joyce reminded her. "She was hoping to see you too."

Lydia was the foster kid her mom had been closest to after her brother had left. They'd spent five years together and she was the nearest Joyce had to a sister. Lydia lived in Seattle but she and her mom had kept in touch, sharing photos of their children as they grew.

"I'd love to see Aunt Lydia," Hayley said. "I hope I'll be home before then, but I can't guarantee it."

"Well, as long as you're back before Christmas," Joyce said. "I don't want to be alone."

"You'll have family on the holiday," Hayley promised. *Maybe more than she expected.*

Chapter Two

B LAKE DENNISON STAMPED the snow off his boots and entered the reception area of Sweetheart Log Homes Limited. Rebel, his black flat-coated retriever, trotted at his heels.

The woodstove in the corner blasted out warmth. Comfy stuffed chairs were placed around a wooden coffee table piled with old copies of *Log Home Living* and a bowl of plastic-wrapped candy canes. Tinny-sounding carols came from the portable radio on a shelf decorated with masses of red garlands and pine cones.

"Hey, Brianna," Blake greeted his boss's daughter, who was hanging another Christmas card on the string tacked to the wall behind her desk. He shrugged out of his sheepskin jacket and draped it over the coat stand next to the door. "New sweater?"

"Like it?" One hand fluffing her dark blonde curls, Brianna struck a pose, proudly showing off a lurid green and red reindeer sweater.

"You should enter the Starr brothers' ugly sweater contest. You'd win, for sure." Blake leafed through the stack of mail piled on the corner of the desk, ready to be distributed. "Have you heard back from Myra about when she's going to stage that spec home? We're running out of time."

"Bad news." Brianna's smile faded. "Her mother broke her hip and needs surgery for a replacement. Myra is going back east to stay with her until she's mobile again."

"I'm sorry about her mom," Blake said. "But the timing couldn't be worse. The ads have already gone in at the realty office and the local papers. Who else is available?"

"I've called all the other staging companies in a two-hundred-mile radius," Brianna said. "Everyone is fully booked."

"Shoot. I wanted that house on the market before Christmas." Blake looked thoughtfully at Brianna. "How are you at decorating?"

"You see my sweater. Do I look as if I have color sense?" Brianna said. "Besides, I don't know anything about staging houses."

"You've seen enough of the end results to be able to figure out the essentials." He gave her a hopeful smile. "Pretty please?"

Brianna held up a hand and averted her gaze. "I'm immune to your puppy dog eyes. Better to show it empty than let me decorate." When he didn't give up, she relented with an elaborate sigh. "I'll try, but I can't guarantee the results."

"You'll do an ace job." Blake picked up his mail and started for his office.

"Dad wants to talk to you as soon as you get in," Brianna said, calling him back. "He's on the phone, but go on in. He said it's important."

Blake poked his head through the door and caught Gordon Renton's eye. His boss, glasses perched atop his thinning gray hair, waved him in and carried on with his phone conversation—with a charity collector by the sounds of it.

Blake wandered over to the window to watch the snow fall steadily on the stacks of yellow cedar logs in the yard. A forklift was moving logs from the pile into the factory shed for bark stripping. The logs were stripped, pre-notched, and made assembly-ready in the factory before being taken onsite.

"Put me down for one hundred dollars," Gordon said to his caller. "No, thank *you* for the great work you do for our young people. Bye now." He hung up.

"You're a generous man, Gordon," Blake said with pride and affection.

"We had a good year, and the youth center is a good cause." Gordon's genial round face creased into a frown as he returned to more worrying business. "I guess you heard about Myra."

"I twisted Brianna's arm, and she said she'd cover," Blake told him. "Any chance Anita would be able to help as well?" Judging by the picture-perfect décor of Gordon's home, his wife, Anita, had the decorating gene that Brianna believed she lacked.

"I'll ask her tonight. We'll figure something out." Gordon waved a hand to a guest chair. "Sit down, Blake."

Blake pulled up a chair in front of Gordon's desk. So there was more on his boss's mind than the problem of getting the spec house staged in time for the open house. "What's up?"

"John Coates called me this morning," Gordon said. "He's putting out feelers to see if I'm interested in selling the company."

"I see." Blake absorbed the unwelcome news. Coates Construction in the nearby town of Polson was their biggest rival, but that wasn't the only problem; he didn't like the underhanded way John Coates did business. "So that explains something Al told me the other day," he said, referring to their factory foreman. "Al ran into a guy from Coates at the hardware wholesaler the other day. Apparently, this guy pumped him for information on the volume of stock we go through annually."

"Coates is trying to gauge how profitable my business is," Gordon said.

"I've heard about his sneaky tactics," Blake said. "He sends out spies to dig for information he can use as leverage when buying someone out. And if they don't sell, Coates launches an aggressive campaign to capture the local market."

"The market for log homes isn't that large that we can withstand his kind of competition," Gordon said. "He has offices in three states, plus he deals in other types of construction besides log homes. He has the bucks to underbid us every time. Eventually, he would drive us out of business. Then I wouldn't be able to sell if I wanted to."

"Our strength is that we're a boutique operation, every home custom designed," Blake said in counterargument. "Plus, Sweetheart Log Homes has a solid reputation and a lot of very satisfied customers. People know you and will vouch for your product. I'd be surprised if Coates could take business away from us."

Gordon shrugged. "New folks moving here don't know me from Adam. They're naturally going to go after the best price."

"Coates cuts corners with inferior products, and the workmanship isn't up to our standards," Blake added. "Sweetheart Log Homes is the best in the business."

"Most people can't tell the difference, or at least not until it's too late." Gordon paused to consider his situation. "Until this is settled one way or another, I don't want you or Brianna talking to anyone about our company or what we're up against."

"That goes without saying," Blake said. "Customer confidence is paramount."

"Anyway, Coates asked for a meeting, and I'd like you to be there," Gordon said.

"You're not seriously thinking of selling, are you?" Blake said, his concern ratcheting up a notch. "This is the first you've mentioned it."

"It hasn't been on my radar," Gordon admitted. "But John's phone call got me to thinking. I'm sixty-five years old. Anita's been after me to retire while I've still got some get up and go. Maybe now is a good time."

Unable to sit still, Blake surged to his feet and paced, struggling to process the thought of Gordon not being at the helm, and of John Coates getting his hands on the business that Blake had helped grow into an award-winning company.

"We're the best log home builders in Montana, maybe the whole west," Blake said. "You've built this business up from nothing and gone from success to success for over forty years. It's part of the fabric of the town."

"I hate the thought of the company going out of the family," Gordon said, his mouth turning down. "But neither of my sons is interested in taking over. Aiden loves teaching and Daniel is doing well at his law firm. If I turn down Coates, I might not get another offer when I want it."

"What about Brianna?" Blake said. "She's smart and capable. She hasn't worked here long, but you started the company with no experience."

"I knew the construction industry. I grew along with the company. It was a lot smaller back then, easier to manage," Gordon said. "Plus, Brianna makes no bones about the fact that she doesn't plan to stay forever. She wants a job in IT. It's what she trained for."

By contrast, Blake did hope to work here forever. He'd started ten years ago while still in high school, stripping the bark from logs in the mill, graduated to a laborer on construction sites during summers home from college, and had gone straight into project management upon graduating with a degree in architecture. He loved his job and the company. He had ideas for their future growth and couldn't picture himself working anywhere else.

"I would buy you out in a heartbeat," Blake said. "But I couldn't wrangle that much cash."

"I wish you could take it over." Gordon took on a thoughtful expression. "Brianna might even stick around if you and she were to, you know, get back together." He rocked a hand suggestively. "Now that Carrie's gone and you're single again."

Oh boy. Gordon was the biggest optimist. Ever since Blake's engagement to his ex-fiancée, Carrie, had ended disastrously, his boss had nurtured the vain hope that Blake and Brianna would make a love match.

"Brianna is terrific." Blake glanced at the open door to the outer office, hoping the radio was drowning out his and Gordon's conversation. He lowered his voice just in case. "I know we dated briefly—two dates, to be exact—but that was years ago." He didn't want to offend Gordon by stating the truth baldly that, while he loved Brianna like a sister, he would never be "in love" with her. Nor she with him. That had been clear to both of them on their first date, confirmed on their second. By mutual consent, there hadn't been a third.

"She's young yet. She could change her mind," Gordon said. "Don't give up hope."

Blake sighed. Brianna was never going to change her mind and fall in love with him. Nor did he want her to. But as long as neither of them were in a committed relationship Gordon would hang on to his misguided hope that one day they would get married, carry on his business, and give him and Anita a bunch of grandchildren. Gordon was a smart dude, but he had this one blind spot.

"Back to Coates Construction," Blake said. "They're a big corporation, and they don't have our town's interests at heart. We employ a lot of locals. When Coates takes over a company, they lay people off. Streamlining, they call it."

"I wouldn't like that any more than you would," Gordon said. "If I sold out, I would try to include a clause about maintaining staff levels."

"Would that be enforceable?" Blake said doubtfully. "Heck, even my job would be on the line."

"I'll talk to Daniel about the legal ramifications," Gordon said.

"This whole conversation feels surreal," Blake said, leaning back in his chair. "I can't even begin to picture you not running this business."

"I can't either, frankly. I haven't made up my mind, by any means," Gordon said. "Anita would love it though. She's been after me to go on that Alaska cruise." He frowned. "Have you ever been on a cruise?"

"I'm not a cruise kind of guy," Blake said. "I'd rather go backpacking in the mountains or on one of Garrett Starr's wilderness adventure trips."

"I'm not sure I'd be into lazing around on a floating restaurant either," Gordon ruminated. "Anyway, a cruise is what, two weeks? What would I do for the other fifty weeks of the year?"

"Golf? Bridge? Stamp collecting?" Blake grinned as Gordon groaned louder with each suggestion. "Okay, never mind. Your problem is, you've always worked too much to develop hobbies."

Gordon conceded that with a nod. "Speaking of work, we'd better get back to it. The building inspector has a query about the house we just finished in Kalispell. Can you give him a call?"

"I'll take care of it this morning." Blake rose. "When are we meeting with Coates?"

"Next week." Gordon consulted his diary. "He said he'd be away from his office Monday and Tuesday on a trip to Sacramento. On Wednesday, Anita and I are going to Marietta for the wedding of our friends' daughter. We'll be away overnight, won't get back till late Thursday. The meeting will have to be next Friday, December 20th."

"I'll keep the date clear. Keep me posted on the time." Blake went back out to the reception area and spoke to Brianna. "Have you got the number for the county building inspector?"

"Sure." She consulted a typed list taped to the wall behind her and wrote it on a notepad. "Are you going to the Starr's Christmas party? It's next Tuesday."

"Wouldn't miss it." Blake took the slip of paper. "Say, did you know John Coates is sniffing around, wanting to buy the company?"

"Yeah, and it sucks," Brianna said. "I don't like him. He acts super friendly; meanwhile, he's circling like a shark. Remember when he took over Flathead Homes? He was so sneaky."

"I remember." Blake shook his head gloomily. "Someone has to do something, or we could all be out of a job."

"You should buy Dad out," Brianna suggested.

"And pigs should fly," Blake said shortly. After Carrie had abruptly left him, he'd poured his life savings into designing and constructing a log home for himself on Finley Point. The house had been a distraction after his life crashed, a consolation prize to look forward to. Gradually, it had become an obsession, and then virtually his whole life. He could sell it and raise the money to buy out Gordon. No, the thought of losing the house now that it was almost finished was unthinkable.

He had started for his office when Brianna called him

back.

"Wait a sec." She glanced at her father's ajar door and lowered her voice. "You should bring a date to the Starr's party so Dad doesn't get any ideas about us."

Blake came closer again and matched her quiet tone. "Could you overhear our conversation?"

She rolled her eyes. "Whenever you guys lower your voices, I know you're talking about me. It doesn't take a genius to figure that out."

"So you know he thinks—"

"I've known it for ages," Brianna said. "He's way off base, so I try not to take any notice. Aside from his bizarre notion about the two of us, I think he's worried about you. It's been over two years since Carrie left, and you're still single."

He felt his expression shutting down. "I date."

"Never the same girl for very long," Brianna pointed out.

The last thing he wanted to discuss was his love life. "Are you inviting someone?"

Brianna smiled slyly and spun back and forth on her chair. "I might."

"Then I don't need to." He cocked a gotcha finger at her and headed for his office, Rebel at his heels.

Chapter Three

I T TOOK HAYLEY a few days to get herself organized to go away, but, by Monday morning, she was driving through a broad, flat valley on her way to the small town of Sweetheart, Montana. Flathead Lake lay to her right; the snow-covered Mission Ranges rose in jagged peaks to her left. A thick layer of snow blanketed the fields and trees but, thankfully, the roads were clear. She cracked the window and sucked in a lungful of fresh air. She'd never been to Montana before, and it was a revelation. So beautiful. A person could breathe out here. She could live here. She really could.

It hadn't been that hard to track down her uncle, thanks to the fact that he owned and ran a business building log homes and had accounts on Facebook, Instagram, and LinkedIn. If her mom wasn't so against social media and, more to the point, so afraid of rejection, she could have found her brother herself.

Hayley slowed as she came to the outskirts of Sweetheart. It was a cute town. No big-box stores or strip malls, just quaint small businesses, cozy cafes and an old-fashioned feel. Bright Christmas decorations hung from lampposts across the streets, and shops had put up their own seasonal touches. Her spirits lifted at the cheery scene. Social media hadn't been able to give her Gordon's home address, but, in a town this size, it shouldn't take long to find her uncle. She couldn't wait to be able to call her mother and tell her the good news.

Her phone rang a few times and stopped. It was her mother. Instead of heading down Main Street, Hayley pulled off the road into Lakeside Park. Three kids were building a snowman, and an older man and woman in thick coats and hats were walking the path by the lake's edge.

Hayley parked and left the car running while she hit the button to call back. While it rang, she glanced at the dashboard clock. Eleven forty-five a.m. No wonder she was getting hungry. "Hi, Mom. I was just thinking about you. Everything okay?"

"Great," Joyce said. "Lydia is arriving this afternoon, and I'm getting a few last-minute things at the supermarket. Where are you? Have you finished your business yet?"

"No, I just got here." She hesitated. "I'm in Montana."

"Montana!" Joyce exclaimed. "I didn't know you did business that far away."

Hayley tapped the wheel with her gloved hand. She didn't want to get her mom's hopes up. Until she'd seen her uncle in person and got a positive response from him about reconciling with her mom, it would be better not to say anything.

"One of my clients is building a log home as a winter vacation retreat," she said, inventing a cover story on the spot. "I'm going to talk to the owner of the construction company and see if he'll show me around some building sites to get ideas for how to decorate. I've never done interiors like these before."

"That sounds interesting. I'm sure you'll do a wonderful job," Joyce said. "I wanted to ask, did you remember to mail my cards?"

"Of course." All except for one. Hayley looked at the envelope resting on the passenger seat with the name Gordon Renton and a stamp, but no address. "Have you been keeping busy?"

"Oh, yes. I had dinner at Bob and Tracey's on Friday, and lunch with my yoga friends yesterday," Joyce said. "I've planned a bunch of things for Lydia and me to do while she's here."

"You have more of a social life than I do." Hayley was glad her mom had lots of friends; it made it easier when she had to be away, especially at this time of year. Especially since Brad wasn't home, either.

"I'm not the one who's a workaholic," her mother said pointedly, then softened. "Kidding. I'm just worried you'll miss seeing Lydia."

"I hope I'll be back, but say hello to her for me," Hayley

said. "I'll call you in a day or two with an update."

"Okay. I'd better run," Joyce said. "Talk soon!"

Hayley said goodbye and left the park, following directions from her GPS to the Montreau Hotel. She carried her suitcase up the steps and entered the spacious lobby of the beautifully restored building. She glanced around appreciatively at the gleaming wood floors, period features, and sparkling chandeliers. Tasteful Christmas decorations added a festive touch.

In the restaurant to her right, men and women in suits and dresses were gathering for a work function. The Annual Western Montana Law Society Christmas party, according to the sandwich board sign at the entrance. To her left was the bar where more casually dressed folks were having lunch.

She carried on to reception and checked in. When she'd finished filling out the form, she asked the young man behind the desk, "Can you tell me where I'd find the office of Sweetheart Log Homes?"

"It's on the outskirts of town, off Mission Range Road." He pulled out a town map from beneath the counter and marked the location of the hotel. "We're here. Go back to Swan and take a left, going away from the lake. A couple of miles past Sweet Street you'll see a company sign. Turn right, go all the way to the end and you'll come to a small industrial park." He beamed at her. "You can't miss it."

"Thanks." She picked up her bag and headed for the elevator. Her last glimpse of the lobby before the doors shut was of people coming and going, everything festive and bustling for Christmas. She could hardly believe she was here, shortly to meet her long-lost uncle for the first time. Her hand pressed her stomach, alive with fluttering butterflies.

The Christmas card was in a side pocket of her purse. She pulled it out and flattened the tiny bend in one corner of the envelope. Had so much ever been riding on a mere greeting card?

Closing her eyes, she said a tiny prayer. *Please, please, please, let my uncle be a kind man and a good brother. Make my mom's Christmas a happy one.*

BLAKE WAS AT his desk working on his latest log home design when he felt his stomach rumble. As if on cue, his boss knocked on his door.

"Want to go to lunch at the Cherry Pit?" Gordon asked. "My treat."

"I'm in." Blake put down his pencil and stretched his arms over his head. After stewing about the possible sale of the company all weekend, he'd come to the conclusion that he needed to convince Gordon to reject John Coates's overtures. No better way to do that than over burgers at the Pit. "But I do believe it's my turn to pick up the tab."

"Nothing doing. I've got the Christmas spirit." Gordon turned to speak to Brianna, who had just emerged from the combination staffroom and kitchen. "Coming to lunch?"

"Thanks, not today. I'm meeting a friend," Brianna said. "Did you answer the accountant's email? I sent him this month's tax receipts, but he asked a question intended for you. He'd like a reply this morning if possible, because he's going away."

"Thanks, Brianna. I'll take care of it now. Be right back, Blake." Gordon headed back to his office.

"Who's your friend?" Blake teased Brianna. "Is he the someone you're going to bring to the Starr's party?"

She tilted her head and grinned. "What makes you think it's a guy?"

"If she was one of your girlfriends you'd mention her name."

Brianna glanced at her father's door. "I'm not sure my dad will approve so I'm keeping him on the down low for now."

Blake frowned. "Gordon only has your welfare in mind. If he wouldn't approve, maybe you shouldn't be going out with this guy."

"No, he's great, honestly," Brianna assured him. "It's just that—"

The outer door opened, and a woman who looked to be in her late twenties entered. She wore a faux fur hat pulled over wavy blonde shoulder-length hair, a red puffy jacket, skinny jeans, and knee-high boots.

Rebel barked, short and sharp, then moved forward to

sniff the newcomer. She bent to pat him. "Hello, gorgeous." Straightening, she nodded to Brianna, and her gaze flickered to Blake. "I'm looking for Gordon Renton?"

Gordon came hurrying out of his office, zipping up his jacket. "Ready to go? I've got a hankering for some cherry pie."

"Dad, this lady is looking for you," Brianna said.

He stopped short, noticing the newcomer. Then extended a hand. "Pleased to meet you. I'm Gordon Renton. What can I do for you?"

"Oh! Hello." For a moment she faltered, seemingly at a loss as to how to proceed. Then she accepted his hand and shook it. "I'm Hayley Stevens."

"My manager, Blake, and my daughter, Brianna, our receptionist and IT person," Gordon said, making the rest of the introductions.

"Nice to meet you all." Hayley shook Brianna's hand and then Blake's.

Blake felt nervousness in the slight tremor of her slender fingers, but his gaze was riveted to her heart-shaped face. Big blue eyes, clear ivory skin with cheeks pink from the cold, a tiny mole to the left of her mouth that drew the gaze to full lips. She reminded him of someone, but he couldn't put his finger on who.

She still hadn't said what she wanted Gordon for.

"How can we help?" Blake said. "Are you interested in purchasing a log home?"

"I beg your pardon? Um, yes, yes, I am," she said with a breathy laugh. "Sorry, I didn't expect to meet Mr. Renton right away. You know, like when you call someone expecting to get voice mail and the person picks up?"

"Well, you got me," Gordon said jovially and spread his arms. "Fire away. What can I do for you?"

Chewing her lower lip, she glanced from Gordon to Blake. "I'm an interior designer. I have my own business in California." She hesitated again and then plunged on. "My…um, that is, one of my clients, is looking for a winter vacation home in Montana. Since I was going to be in the area, I said I'd check some out for her." Hayley took in their coats. "I was hoping to discuss her needs over lunch, but I can see you're on your way somewhere."

"Lunch is where we're headed. You're welcome to join us." Gordon turned to Blake. "Okay with you?"

What could he say? His anti-Coates campaign would have to wait. "Sure, that would be great."

Outside, there was a short confusion over whose car to take. They finally settled on Blake driving his four-wheel drive truck with Gordon in the passenger seat and Hayley in the back with Rebel because the dog went everywhere with him. Blake worried about dog hair getting on her clothes but Hayley insisted she didn't mind. At least she wasn't a princess, a point in her favor in Blake's opinion.

"I hope you don't mind a diner," Blake said to Hayley as he pulled onto the road into town. "The dining room at the

Montreau Hotel is booked out today. Bunch of legal eagles getting together."

"I know," Hayley said. "I just came from there."

"My son, Daniel, is at that lunch," Gordon said and then went on to tell Blake that Daniel had just been made partner in the town's main law firm.

"I'll bet he was glad to get the news before Christmas," Blake said.

Hayley added, "You must be very proud of your son."

"Oh, I am. He's worked hard for this." Gordon went on to tell their visitor about Daniel's career to date.

Blake smiled indulgently. His boss was gregarious, and there was nothing he liked better than to talk about his family.

A few minutes later, they pulled into a diagonal parking slot in front of the diner. Blake held the restaurant door open for Hayley.

"Thanks." As she entered, she took off her hat and shook out the tumble of wavy honey-blonde hair. By chance, she looked up and their eyes met. A spark, brief and potent, passed between them.

Automatically, he started to follow, as if pulled by the floral note that floated on the air around her. Gordon, waiting to enter, cleared his throat and gave him an amused look. Blake stepped back, his neck heating at being caught eyeing their new client. Potential client. Clearly, she'd impressed him, but they still had to impress her.

"I hope you didn't mind the personal chat on the way over here," Gordon said as they settled around a table by the window. "It's a small town, so we're pretty informal. Everyone knows everyone, and the names of all their dogs."

"Not at all," she began eagerly. "In fact, I—" Then with a glance at Blake, she checked herself. "I like learning about the people behind the product. I always tell my clients that the more you know about the provenance of what you're buying the more certain you can be that you're getting quality."

"Then you've come to the right place," Blake said. "Sweetheart Log Homes is known for quality."

"If we do say so ourselves," Gordon added modestly.

Skye, the waitress, strode over, ponytail swinging, to drop off menus and fill their coffee cups. "Hey, Gordon, Blake." She nodded a friendly hello to Hayley. "Specials today are roast turkey with mashed potatoes and gravy, and vegetarian lasagna."

"I'll have my usual, Skye," Gordon said. To Hayley he added, "The burgers here are excellent."

"Turkey for me," Blake said, handing over his menu.

"The lasagna sounds good," Hayley said.

Skye collected the menus. "Coming right up."

When she'd left, Hayley asked, "Sweetheart is an interesting name for a town. Where did that come from?"

"Did you notice all the cherry orchards as you drove into town?" Blake said. "They were planted after the Second

World War by a returning soldier, Nathan Starr. 'Sweetheart' is the type of cherry he grew."

"Nathan is still around, though he's getting on a bit," Gordon added. "His son is Robert Starr, the local Realtor. Robert's log home is one of the first I built, over forty years ago."

"You've been in business a long time then," Hayley said to Gordon. "I'm impressed. What made you set up in Sweetheart? Are you from the area?"

"No, I'm from California originally but I traveled around some then found Flathead Lake," Gordon said. "I liked the town, the outdoor lifestyle, the open spaces. I'd worked in construction. Figured log homes would be a good fit for both me and the town."

"What type of log home is your client interested in?" Blake asked.

"She's…not sure," Hayley said. "That's part of what I'm here to investigate." She turned back to Gordon. "So you have two grown children, Daniel and Brianna? It's nice that they live close by."

"Three children," Gordon corrected. "My other son, Aiden, is a teacher."

"Does he live in Sweetheart too?"

"That's right," Gordon said. "They all went away to college for a few years, but once they settled down, they came back."

"I guess they have aunts and uncles and cousins here,

too, don't they?" Hayley plucked a sugar packet from the bowl and casually flipped it between her fingers.

Blake watched. There was that slight tremor in her hands again.

"Not really," Gordon replied. "My wife's family is from the East Coast. They all settled in Massachusetts and Connecticut."

"You don't have brothers or sisters yourself?" Hayley stopped flipping and clutched the thin paper packet.

Gordon went very still. Blake glanced from him to Hayley, who waited with an oddly intense attentiveness for his answer.

"I have no family," Gordon said shortly.

Blake frowned. "I thought you had a sister somewhere."

"Our lunch is taking a long time." Gordon swiveled to look toward the serving window where the cook could be seen at the grill. When he turned back, his face had closed down completely.

"I'm sure Anita mentioned her once," Blake said, not understanding his boss's strange reaction.

"We lost touch with each other a long time ago," Gordon replied.

"That's a shame," Blake murmured. And very strange. He knew how important family was to Gordon. He'd just assumed Gordon saw his sister occasionally. For him to deny his only sibling, the rift must have been bad.

Hayley had put the sugar packet back in the bowl, and

her hands clasped each other tightly. Her face was pale. Blake sent her an apologetic smile, but her gaze was cast down. She'd probably had no idea when she'd innocently asked after Gordon's family that she was stumbling into a minefield of sibling rivalry or whatever it was that had come between Gordon and his sister.

Although, come to think of it, why had Hayley probed so hard? Making conversation was one thing, but, surely, Gordon's personal life had no bearing on whether her client bought a house from him.

"You'll have to forgive me if I seemed nosy," Hayley said to Gordon, although her gaze included Blake. "I love small towns. I think it's amazing how generation after generation stay in the same place and build a community. The returned soldier, the cherry orchards…there's so much history and interconnected families. I'm interested in all that."

"Don't worry about it," Gordon said, but his normally genial expression was still uncharacteristically dour.

An awkward silence fell over the table.

"Are you familiar with the different types of log homes?" Blake asked Hayley to break the tension.

"Not as much as I'd like to be." With an expression of relief, she turned her attention to him. "Please tell me."

"Full scribe, post and beam, and timber frame or hybrid," Blake explained. "We have a brochure back at the office, or you can look on our website for more details." He spent the next few minutes describing the basic differences between construction methods. Hayley nodded along, although he wasn't sure she was taking it all in.

Skye returned then, bringing their food. By the time she'd refilled their coffees and gone again, the atmosphere had returned to normal. Almost normal. Gordon was unusually quiet, and Hayley still looked pale.

"What does your client do?" Blake asked Hayley, determined to bring the conversation back to the purpose of their lunch. "How big a home is she looking for?"

Again, Hayley hesitated, almost as if she had to think up an answer on the spot. "She is, was…a nurse practitioner. She's retired now."

Blake glanced at Gordon to see if he wanted to jump in, but he was concentrating on eating his burger. Would they still be a company long enough to build this woman's house, should she choose to go with them?

"Does she plan to sell her home in California and move to Montana?" Blake asked. He didn't know offhand how much nurse practitioners made, but log homes didn't come cheap, and not many people could afford to keep two houses for only one person. On the other hand, they could build to a client's budget. And some people just liked looking. If Hayley's client wasn't a serious buyer, he'd like to know up front.

"I…don't know her future plans," Hayley said. "She wants a place she can come to, to be with family."

"Is she looking for acreage or something in town?" Blake

went on. "It would help to know her price range."

Hayley bit her lip and, again, Blake could almost see the wheels turning. Strange sort of consultant who didn't do her leg work. Had she really come all the way from California on a house-buying mission without having the basic details figured out?

A sudden thought occurred to him that made his mouth go dry. Had she been hired by John Coates to grill them for any weak spots? Their rival was notorious for the lengths he would go to to get what he wanted. Blake took a sip of water. Surely he was being paranoid. Bringing someone in from three states away was too big a stretch even for Coates. Wasn't it? And yet Gordon said Coates had just gone to Sacramento.

"She has no idea of the market and, frankly, neither do I," Hayley admitted. "Part of my brief is to find out what's available and report back."

"You might have saved yourself a trip if you'd looked at our website first," Blake said. "There's information there about log homes in general and lots of photos, as well as sample floor plans."

"Oh, I did see all that," she said. "I came across the Facebook page for Sweetheart Log Homes, and that led me to your website. But there's a world of difference between looking at photos online and actually seeing the house in person."

"True," Blake had to concede.

"I'm sure we can accommodate your client's needs whatever they are," Gordon said. "We build houses in a wide range of style and price, from luxury mansion to rustic cabin. Blake's even working on a design for a tiny home. He can fill you in on all that."

"I'll be checking out another company in the area too," she said, almost as an afterthought. "Coates Construction, I think it's called, in Polson."

Blake exchanged a glance with Gordon. "Coates is well-known, but they're very big. You won't get the individualized service that we provide. We're one of the few companies that build log homes all the way from design to construction to ready for occupancy."

"That's right," Gordon said. "We're a family business with the personal touch. But don't listen to us blow our own horn. See for yourself. We have a recently completed spec home that you can view."

"That would be wonderful," Hayley said to him. "Would you be able to show me through yourself?"

"I'd be glad to." Having apparently recovered his good humor, Gordon wiped a last french fry through the ketchup and popped it in his mouth.

"Excuse me, Gordon," Blake said. "Not to put a crimp in things, but you and Anita are going to Marietta on Wednesday, and Brianna rearranged your schedule. You're busy all day today and tomorrow."

"Yes, you're right," Gordon said. "Could you take Hayley around?"

Blake was tempted to suggest Brianna do it. Hayley's arrival was an unexpected distraction when he wanted to concentrate on figuring out how to prevent Coates Construction from buying out the company. But it wasn't Brianna's job, and he could answer any technical questions Hayley might have. If Sweetheart Log Homes was going to survive, it wouldn't hurt to have more work lined up.

"I'd be happy to show you the house," he said to Hayley. "How is tomorrow morning, first thing?"

Was it his imagination or did her expression falter briefly? With no false modesty, young women didn't usually prefer Gordon to himself. Had he only imagined there'd been a spark earlier when their eyes had met? Maybe Brianna was right—he'd been single too long. Had he lost his ability to decipher a woman's signals?

"Thank you, that would be fine," Hayley said. "I appreciate your time."

Gordon glanced at his watch. "If you two will excuse me, I'm going to drop in at the Realtor and have a quick chat with Robert about the ad for the spec house. Blake, I'll find my own way back to the office." He turned to Hayley. "I hope you enjoy your stay in Sweetheart, Ms. Stevens. I know Blake will take good care of you, but if you have any more questions, my door is always open."

"Thank you," she said, smiling warmly. "It was so nice to meet you." She reached for her wallet.

Gordon waved away Hayley's offer to pay for her own lunch and took care of the bill. They parted on the sidewalk out front, Gordon to walk across the road to Starr Realty, Blake to escort Hayley back to his truck. She sat up front this time, much to Rebel's disappointment.

"Lie down." Blake shooed him away when he poked his head between them, tongue hanging out and panting. "Sorry," he said to Hayley. "He thinks he's a person."

"He's adorable," Hayley said, getting in a pat before the dog obediently settled on the floor. When they were on the road, she asked Blake, "Have you lived in Sweetheart long?"

"My mom was from here originally," he told her. "When she married my father, they lived in Bozeman, but she moved back after he passed away."

"I'm so sorry," she murmured.

"It was a long time ago. He was killed in Iraq when I was only a toddler." Blake was able to relate the facts without emotion, but that didn't mean he hadn't missed having a father growing up. "Like Gordon's kids, I went away to college and then came back. I figure this is paradise, so why would I go anywhere else?" He turned off Swan Street onto the industrial park road. "Where are you from?"

"I live in San Diego," Hayley said.

"Is your family there?" Blake asked.

"My mom lives in Fallbrook, about an hour north of the city and inland. My brother is in San Clemente, which is also quite near, but we don't see him much."

"Oh?" Blake said, curious about the slight edge in her voice when she spoke of her brother.

"He goes overseas for work a lot," Hayley said. "He's away right now, in the Philippines." She paused. "I don't know if he'll be back for Christmas."

Hearing the hint of sadness in her voice, Blake said, "You and your mom must miss him." There was something else there too—frustration, annoyance?

"We miss him a lot. My father died earlier this year. There's only the three of us now." She looked out the window at the snow-covered fields. Blake heard a quiet sniff and kept his gaze straight ahead. Then she turned back with an embarrassed laugh. "Sorry, this time of year makes me feel sentimental. I miss my dad. And I didn't get a chance to say goodbye to my brother, Brad, or wish him a merry Christmas."

"I'm sure your brother will do his best to be back so you can say it in person," Blake said, feeling the inadequacy of the response.

Back at the office, he went inside to get Hayley a stack of brochures and information pamphlets. When he came back out she was standing by her car. As he handed her the folder, he cast an eye over her all-weather tires—fine for light snow, but not designed for a Montana winter.

"More snow is forecast for later this week," he said. "In case you were planning on being around that long."

"I'm not sure how long I'll be here," she said. "I guess as

long as it takes. My car is all-wheel drive," she added a trifle defensively.

"Just want to be sure you get where you're going," he said. "Brand's Auto on Fourth Avenue can fix you up with chains if necessary."

"Thanks for your concern," she said. "And for the brochures. I'll look them over this afternoon and meet you here in the morning. How is nine a.m.?"

"It's good. See you then." Blake shook her hand again. This time there was no tremor, just soft skin and a firm warm grip. Her blonde hair gleamed in the winter sunlight, and her blue eyes were warm and friendly. If she was a distraction, she was a pleasant one.

But, as she drove away, he couldn't shake the niggling feeling that all was not as it seemed with Hayley.

Chapter Four

HAYLEY DROVE BACK to Sweetheart feeling bad about the elaborate story she'd spun to explain her presence there. When she'd conceived of the idea of going to her uncle's business place, she'd imagined being ushered into his private office. With Blake and Brianna standing right there, she'd felt put on the spot and hadn't wanted to blurt out who she was. And if she'd done that in front of the others, she would have put Gordon on the spot. So she'd invented a mythical client looking for a log home. From there, the story had grown. It was going to be tricky when she had to confess she was actually his niece.

But, oh, how could her uncle have said he had no family? Only to then admit under duress that he had a sister but imply that he didn't wish to renew her acquaintance. For a stunned second, Hayley had wondered if she was talking to the wrong Gordon Renton. But he couldn't be. Even though he was decades older than in the photo booth picture, there was no mistaking the shape of his nose and the mole on his cheek. She touched the beauty mark on her own cheek and felt her throat clog. She was his niece even if he didn't know it. They were family.

And now he was going away on Wednesday and would be busy right up until then. When was she going to get to see him alone?

When she'd bid him goodbye after lunch, feeling as if her insides were cracking open, she'd found it hard to smile. What had happened all those years ago to drive him to cut ties with her mom? There had to be more to the story than her mother knew, or was telling her. Whatever the problem was, the wound had caused a rift that had never healed for her uncle. What she couldn't figure out was whether he was angry or sad. His face had gone so blank, it was impossible to read him. And once he'd gone off to see the Realtor, she'd lost any opportunity to corner him alone after lunch.

Blake was a puzzle, too, albeit a really attractive one. Thick black hair, a cleft in his chin, full mouth, and sculptured cheeks and jaw. Just thinking about the zing of attraction when he'd held the restaurant door for her and she'd looked straight into his dreamy dark eyes made her melt all over again. But as lunch had progressed, she'd gotten the distinct feeling that he was scrutinizing her almost suspiciously. More than once, she'd seen a puzzled frown on his face as she spoke. Had she been too obviously interested in her uncle?

Blake appeared protective of Gordon, which she admired, but it wasn't clear why her uncle should need shields placed around him. He was a successful, confident businessman, no doubt more than capable of looking after himself. She tried to tell herself it didn't matter what Blake thought of her, as long as he didn't interfere with her mission, but it *did* matter. She'd only just met him, but already she liked him, and could see he was a really genuine person. For him to show her houses when she had no client interested in buying, would be a waste of his time, but she didn't see how she could get out of it now.

Although, after glimpsing a few houses on the internet, she was curious about learning more about log homes. They seemed so perfectly suited for the rugged Montana landscape she'd taken an instant liking to.

She peered out at the sky. Thick gray clouds were building on the horizon. It would be terrible to get stuck here in a snowstorm and miss Christmas with her mom. The thought of driving in snow was scary. Once she'd hit ice going through the mountains in Northern California, and she'd almost gone head-on into an oncoming semitrailer. That had been enough to terrify her out of ever driving in the snow again.

Chains were the answer. She drove over to Fourth Avenue and found Brand's Auto. It was a small, independent garage, the kind she liked to patronize, but it was busy, so she kept going. She could come back later. And, who knows, the weatherman could be wrong, or she could be finished here before snow came.

Heading back down Main Street to the hotel, she noticed that Swan Street had been blocked off for a Christmas market. That might be fun to look around. She already had Christmas presents for her mom, Brad, and a few friends, but there was Gordon and his family.

She parked at the hotel and wound her scarf around her neck, preparing to walk back to the market. Before she got out of the car, she pulled out her phone. She still hadn't talked to Brad since the day he'd called from the airport. Hearing Gordon speak so dismissively of her mother made her want to make contact with her brother before any bad feelings between them grew bigger.

A quick mental calculation told her it would be around four a.m. in Manila. Brad had always been a night owl and insomniac. Factor in jet lag and he might be awake. Sitting there with her fingers poised over his name on her speed dial, a faint burn of resentment tainted her desire to hear his voice. At the airport, Brad hadn't remembered for two minutes that she'd wanted to speak to him again. It seemed as if she was always the one making the effort to stay in touch, arranging visits, sending emails.

He was helping save lives, she reminded herself. But family mattered too. He'd promised, on his honor, that he would be home this year. Only last week they'd talked about making this first Christmas without their father as happy as possible for their mother. Mom had lots of good friends, but what she really wanted was to be with her children at Christmas.

Hayley blew out a frustrated sigh. Was she being ungenerous by feeling annoyed with Brad? Well, yes, she probably was. Those poor people devastated by the typhoon needed all the help they could get. It took selfless folks like her brother to rush to their aid. And yet…a tiny part of her couldn't help feeling hurt. Brad didn't have to go this time. It almost felt like he'd chosen to be with strangers rather than spend Christmas with her and Mom. Did he prefer the excitement of being in the thick of the rescue effort to the more staid pleasures of a holiday with her and Mom?

Surely not. But she was no longer in the mood to chat with him. Putting her phone back in her purse, and her uncharitable thoughts out of her mind, she left the car and headed down the street to the market.

As she walked, her thoughts returned to her uncle. When she'd hinted to her mom that Gordon hadn't been the nicest brother, Joyce had defended him warmly. Hayley's first impressions of her uncle were of a kindly, generous man, but sometimes people put on a front. Before she came clean about who she was, it would be a good idea to find out what people who knew Gordon Renton well thought of him.

She crossed the road and found herself among brightly colored market umbrellas. The spicy scents of the season wafted from tasting stalls and her mood lifted as she browsed her way slowly down the street. There were so many beautiful handcrafted gifts that it was difficult to choose. She bought whatever took her fancy as presents for her long-lost family—a wooden cheese board, ceramic pots filled with scented candles, homemade soap, handcrafted chocolates. She enjoyed imagining the surprise and pleasure on their faces when they opened them.

A banner proclaiming Starr Orchards drew her over to the stall where a simmering Crock-Pot gave off a delicious aroma of cherries. An attractive fifty-something woman muffled to her chin in a bright fuchsia scarf ladled mulled wine into a tiny paper cup and handed it to Hayley.

Hayley sipped cautiously, and a delicious, spicy flavor filled her mouth. "Oh, my goodness."

"What do you think?" the woman asked. "A bit different, isn't it?"

"It's amazing," Hayley enthused. "What's that taste, I mean besides cherry? I can't put my finger on it, but it's heavenly."

"There's the usual cinnamon and nutmeg, but the spice that makes it special is star anise. I put it in the jam too." The woman winked. "Don't tell anyone. My friend Sarah put me on to it. Now it's a trade secret."

Hayley mimed zipping her lip. "I'll take three bottles and three jars of jam." These were for Mom, Brad, and herself. No doubt Gordon's family was already familiar with the Starr's products.

The woman processed her order and placed the bottles

into paper bags. "Haven't seen you around before. Are you in town for the holidays?"

"I'm here for a few days, maybe longer. It depends." She could see the questions in the woman's gaze but also that she was too polite to pry. "I'm looking at real estate, log homes in particular," Hayley added.

"My husband Robert is the local Realtor. I'm Linda." She handed Hayley the bag with a smile. "His office is just down the street. Starr Realty. You should drop in and see if he has any listings you'd be interested in."

"Thanks, but the client I'm representing is more interest-ed in building a new home." How easily that little embellishment had tripped off her tongue. She'd said it so she wouldn't have to repeat her made-up story to Robert Starr, but in doing so, she'd added another layer to her fictional client. She wouldn't be surprised if her nose was growing.

"I'm Hayley Stevens, by the way." She put her hand out and shook Linda's. "I was out at Sweetheart Log Homes this morning. I just had lunch with Gordon and Blake."

"You can't go wrong with them," Linda said warmly. "They're very reputable builders. Gordon built our log home decades ago, and it's still as solid as a rock."

"That's good to know." Hayley picked up a jar of com-pote and studied the label. "He seems like a nice man."

"He's the best," Linda agreed. "He sits on the Chamber of Commerce with Robert and he sponsors a Little League team. You can always count on Gordon."

Hayley wanted to ask for more details but worried that might sound weird coming from a stranger. This was a small town, and she'd already made Blake wary with her questions. "Well, thanks again."

Turning away, she was startled to find herself face-to-face with the young woman who had been behind the reception desk at Sweetheart Log Homes. Hayley recognized the lurid reindeer sweater peeking out below a flowered jacket. "Hi…Brianna, isn't it?"

"Yes. Hayley, right?" Brianna's wide smile was infectious. "How was lunch? I hope Dad and Blake didn't bore you to death with log home specs. The stuff they know about wood could fill an encyclopedia. Have you been trying Linda's cherry products?" she rattled on. "They're awesome."

Hayley held up her bag. "I almost bought out the stall."

"Did you try the cherry compote with cheddar cheese?" Brianna asked.

"I must have missed that."

"Linda, can we—" Brianna began, but Linda was already preparing crackers with cheddar and cherry compote.

Hayley took a bite. "Oh, my goodness, this is fabulous." She gave Linda a rueful smile. "Guess I'll have to have a jar of the compote as well."

"This one is on the house," Linda said, handing her a jar. She glanced from Hayley to Brianna. "You two have almost exactly the same color of hair, although Brianna's is curlier.

And the same blue eyes. Isn't that funny. You could almost be sisters."

"Really, you think so?" Hayley's heart began to race. She studied Brianna who was doing the same to her.

"Except that my blonde hair came out of a bottle, so that ruins that theory," Brianna said, laughing. "I actually have light brown hair like my dad used to before he went gray," she confided to Hayley. "I wouldn't mind having a sister though. My two older brothers tease me to death. The torture I put up with!"

"You know you adore them," Linda chided good-naturedly. "And they dote on you."

"They're pretty great most of the time," Brianna conceded.

"Are you coming to our party tomorrow?" Linda asked Brianna. "We're having it midweek because this time of year is so busy."

"Sure am," Brianna said, and turned to Hayley. "You should come too."

"Oh, no, I couldn't. I'm…a stranger." Embarrassed, Hayley flicked a glance at Linda with an apologetic smile.

"Strangers are simply friends we haven't gotten to know yet," Linda said cheerfully. "Brianna's family are good friends and, since you're here to do business with them, we'd love for you to come too. Five to seven p.m. We're north of town on Finley Road. Big sign out front saying Starr Orchards. You can't miss it."

"Thank you, if you're sure," Hayley said. "That would be lovely." Her spirits lifted as she realized her uncle was bound to be there. The party might be her only opportunity to tell him who she was and give him the Christmas card from her mom.

"Don't dress up; dress warmly," Brianna advised. "They do sleigh rides through the orchard."

"That's definitely something to look forward to," Hayley said. "I've never been on a sleigh ride before."

Brianna bought a bottle of cherry wine and a bag of the spices that went with it. "Thanks, Linda. Come on, Hayley. You've got to try the hot chocolate from Lynn's café. And then there's the bratwurst that Pete Webber makes from his own pigs."

"Sounds delicious, but I just had lunch," Hayley protested.

"So did I," Brianna said. "Just a taste, I promise."

Hayley waved to Linda over her shoulder and followed Brianna through the crowded pedestrian walk. "People here sure are friendly."

"Aren't they where you come from?" Brianna asked curiously.

"Well, yes, but here you all seem extra nice." With the possible exception of Blake. What exactly *did* he think of her? She would love to know.

"Have my dad and Blake talked you into buying a house yet?" Brianna asked. "We have a spec home for sale out of town, but I've got to warn you, it's not staged yet. Our stager had a family emergency."

"Blake's taking me to view it tomorrow," Hayley replied. "I'm sorry to hear it's not decorated. Log homes are so different from anything I've dealt with before. I'm not sure I'd know where to begin."

"Well, you probably wouldn't want to go too dainty," Brianna said. "People do western furnishings mostly around here. *Avant-garde* can work well, too, with the right touch."

She stopped at the hot chocolate stall and ordered two cups. Hayley paid, ignoring Brianna's objections.

"Western sounds fun," Hayley said, sipping the velvety drink as they walked slowly through the stalls. "I suppose there's lots of that around?"

"Antiques Barn up on Route 35 has everything you could possibly need, from furniture to linen to paintings." Brianna turned to her suddenly with a hopeful smile. "You're an interior designer, right?" Hayley nodded. "You wouldn't want a job while you're here, would you? We want to get that house on the market before Christmas. The job of staging it has fallen to me, and I'm hopeless at decorating."

"Oh, well, I—" Hayley floundered. Did she have time? It would give her an opportunity to do something for her uncle and a legitimate reason to stick around town until he returned. Plus, it would be an opportunity to get to know her cousin better. *And Blake.* She pushed that thought aside. Last but not least, she could find out more about log homes. The more she learned, the more she wanted to know. She wished she did have a client just so she could work with the homes.

"Sorry, don't pay any attention to me," Brianna said, quickly backpedaling when Hayley hesitated. "I was only kidding. You don't want to get ambushed into another job when you're here for your client."

"What's your time frame?" Hayley asked. "I'm not going to be here very long."

"This week?" Brianna said hopefully. "It doesn't have to be elaborate, just a couch and some pictures on the wall."

"Oh, I think we can do better than that," Hayley said. "I'd be happy to stage your spec home. I'm always looking for ways to expand my business. This would give me something new to put in my portfolio."

"Awesome!" Brianna said. "I knew I liked you the moment I saw you."

Hayley smiled at her cousin's enthusiasm. She liked Brianna too. It was impossible not to. "Where did you say the Antiques Barn is located?"

"It's about an hour north of here on Route 35," Brianna said. "I'll come with you. I love antique shopping. I could be your assistant."

"That would be great," Hayley said.

"And you will come to the party tomorrow, won't you?" Brianna said. "Linda meant it when she invited you."

"You didn't give her much choice." Hayley's mouth twisted to soften the gentle chastisement. "She was probably just being polite."

"No, she's really hospitable, honestly," Brianna assured her. "It'll be fun. Better than sitting in your hotel room, wishing you were at home with your family."

What would happen if Hayley came out right now and told Brianna who she was? She would likely be thrilled. A girl cousin was almost as good as a sister. On the other hand, she seemed impulsive and talkative. She might rush straight to her father and drop the bombshell. If he was busy or not in a good mood, he might react negatively. After what happened in the diner, Hayley was now doubly cautious. For a man who wouldn't acknowledge he had a sister, the timing when he found out she was his niece had to be just right.

The Starr's party would be a festive occasion, a genial gathering of friends and family. What better opportunity to meet her aunt and her other cousins, Daniel and Aiden, and to get to know her uncle in a social situation?

"All right, if you really think I wouldn't be intruding, I'd like very much to come," Hayley said. "Thank you for including me."

"No worries." Brianna nudged her with a wink. "Sis."

Chapter Five

HAYLEY WOKE EARLY the next morning. Over a room service breakfast of fresh fruit and a muffin, she looked at the brochure Blake had given her. While poring over the technical details last night, her fascination with the method of building had grown. The photos of homes the company had built were nothing short of stunning. She'd stayed up late, researching log homes on the internet and studying the décor. It was actually a stroke of luck getting the opportunity to stage the spec home. She might not have a client with plans to build now but with this under her belt she would have a better chance of attracting one. Plus it had been a while since she'd felt the thrill of a new challenge.

Last night's clouds had disappeared and this morning the snow-capped mountains were etched sharply against a brilliant blue sky. When she pulled into the log home company parking lot a few minutes before nine, Blake was leaning against his truck, scrolling through his phone while he waited.

Hearing her car, he straightened and put his phone away, then walked over to meet her. She got out, enjoying the few seconds she had to admire his long-legged stride and broad shoulders. His head was bare this morning and his dark hair lifted in the slight breeze, ruffled into waves.

She handed him a coffee. "White, no sugar."

His bark of laughter puffed out condensation in the chilly air. "You must have been taking notes yesterday at lunch."

"I'm observant, by nature and by training," she said, pleased to have surprised him. "Knowing your client, attention to detail—they're a big part of my job."

"I thought you were *our* client. But thanks." He lifted his cup in salute. "I was running late this morning and didn't get a chance to grab my own coffee." His eyes narrowed humorously. "Maybe you already knew that."

Hayley's turn to laugh. "I'm not that good. Anyway, you are my client now. I told Brianna yesterday that I would stage your spec home. If you and Gordon agree, of course."

Blake's eyebrows rose. "Is that right? Well, that's wonderful. Are you sure you'll have time? Aren't you here for your own work?"

"The two things will combine perfectly," she said. "I have to warn you, though, I've never done a log home. It'll be a learning experience, one that I hope to be able to draw on for my own business in the future. Another string to add to my bow." She dug in her purse for a business card and handed him one. "You can check out my website."

"Oh, I've already checked you out," he said, a small smile playing around his mouth. "You'll do just fine."

Her stomach fluttered, and she was momentarily lost for words.

"When did you talk to Brianna about the house?" Blake asked, filling the awkward gap in the conversation.

"I ran into her at the Christmas market yesterday," Hayley said. "She invited me to go with her to the Antiques Barn when she shops for furnishings for the staging. She half-jokingly asked if I would consider taking on the job. I think she was quite surprised when I agreed, but pleased."

"I'm sure she's thrilled. The woman who usually does our staging had to cancel at the last minute, so Brianna was a little freaked out at being landed with the task," Blake said. "She can code like a Silicon Valley nerd, but her design sense leaves something to be desired. I suspect she might even be color blind."

"She does have eclectic taste," Hayley agreed diplomatically. Then she shivered. "Should we go? It's a tad chilly to stand around the parking lot."

"You call this chilly?" Blake glanced around as if surprised. "It's positively balmy."

"Oh, yeah, it's practically spring," Hayley said dryly. Fir trees dusted with snow ringed the far border of the property. Icicles hung from the eaves of all the buildings. Except where the parking lot and driveways and paths had been shoveled, the ground was covered in white. With an exaggerated shiver, she huddled further into her jacket and turned up the collar. "It's freezing."

"You can ride along with me again," Blake said, still with that teasing gleam in his eye. "Not sure I trust your sissy West Coast car in the snow."

"Sissy?" she repeated, pretending outrage because it was impossible not to respond. "I'll have you know my car made it through a Northern California snowstorm. Although I'm sure your big bruiser of a truck will enjoy the opportunity to show off."

Chuckling, he opened the passenger door for her. "I hope you don't mind that it's me and not Gordon showing you around."

There was the tiniest edge to his voice. What was that about? Had he guessed that she'd given them a cover story, or was that being paranoid? She would have liked to confide in Blake, just as she longed to talk to Brianna. To have allies on her side when she broached her uncle would make a huge difference. But if Gordon didn't want to know his sister, then his loyal employee would no doubt stand by him, even run interference. Was that what Blake was doing now? Yesterday, he'd been awfully quick to remind Gordon that he didn't have time to show Hayley around.

"Why would I mind?" she countered with a bright smile, hoping that he would answer and tell her what he was really thinking.

"Oh, I don't know." He climbed in behind the wheel.

"Maybe you think the head of the company would know more about the log homes than a mere underling."

"You don't strike me as an underling." She settled into her seat and did up the buckle. "I have no doubt you'll be able to answer all my questions." Her gaze lingered a moment on his strong profile. Having Gordon show her the houses would have suited her purposes better, but there were worse things than being squired around town by this hunk of a builder.

BLAKE DROVE DOWN Mission Range Road toward the highway, very aware of Hayley sitting next to him in the passenger seat. Her slender, expressive hands were folded tidily in her lap, giving an aura of calm, but those bright blue eyes roamed the landscape, taking in every detail of her surroundings. Long legs encased in tight jeans stretched under the dash. Every time she swiveled to look at something, her elusive floral scent wafted his way, eliciting crazy thoughts of burying his nose in her hair.

"I appreciate you doing this," Hayley said. "You probably had other plans for today."

He turned onto Route 35 in the northbound lane along the lakeshore. "Nothing that can't keep," he replied easily.

"I guess winter is slower for house construction here," she hazarded.

"Not necessarily," he replied. "With new techniques, we can build all year round. In fact, there are some advantages to starting a home in winter, as long as you do appropriate site preparation. Anyway, there's more to what we do than simply building the homes." He cast her a sidelong glance. "But you would know that, being in business yourself."

"True," she said. "There's planning, buying, marketing, accounting. All that takes a lot of time, especially when you're small and do most of it yourself." She paused. "Are you and Gordon the only management?"

Blake nodded agreement without elaborating. Sweetheart Log Homes was coming to a crossroads, but the possibility of the company changing hands wasn't something he would talk about with a prospective client. Especially an interior designer who might bring more work their way in the future. If they were still in business come the new year.

Everything was up in the air right now, and he didn't like the atmosphere of uncertainty. He liked to feel solid, grounded. It was bad enough that his personal life had gone through a period of turmoil over the past couple of years. Going to work every day, doing the best job he knew how, channeling his energies into building his own log home in his spare time, all these things had gotten him through his breakup with Carrie. For Gordon now to be considering selling the company, well, it threw Blake back into the eye of the storm, so to speak.

How serious was Hayley's client about buying a log

home? Part of him wanted to warn her that if she went ahead and contracted with Sweetheart Log Homes to build a house, the man who signed the deal might not be the same person who saw the project through to the end. If Coates Construction took over Blake couldn't even guarantee he would be around. But he didn't want to send out signals that they couldn't deliver; that would be sure to drive business away.

And, too, there was the niggling knowledge at the back of his mind that John Coates sent out spies to get information about companies he wanted to buy. He glanced at Hayley again, but her straight nose, full lips the color of ripe raspberries and thick brown lashes gave nothing away. She looked more like a hot version of the girl next door than a spy. But weren't spies good at disguise?

"Is it usual for an interior designer to give the kind of service you offer, coming all the way to Montana just before Christmas?" he asked.

"I wouldn't do it for everyone," she admitted. "This client is special."

"A celebrity?" he guessed.

Smiling, she shook her head.

"A relative then?"

Hayley hesitated. "Something like that."

His instincts told him she was hiding something, but he had no idea what. By "a relative" could she be referring to Coates? She might be a daughter or a niece. He tried to recall what he knew of Coates's family and came up blank. Hayley could even be a friend of the family, for that matter.

"How many homes does your company sell in a year?" she asked.

He almost balked at answering, but it was a fair question. One test of how good a company was could be based on sales. "Depends on the year, but we average twenty to thirty."

"That sounds more like a range than an average."

"Can't be more specific, sorry." He smiled blandly. "We do okay. Haven't had to lay off anyone this winter, and that's a good thing."

"That is good," she agreed.

She was from San Diego and had the California license plates on her car to prove it which suggested she wasn't connected to Coates. On the other hand, Coates was in Sacramento right now. Rumor had it he was starting a new office out west.

As they drove past a house on acreage, a man and a woman on cross-country skis left their backyard, went through a gate, and headed off across a snow-covered field.

"Oh, look," Hayley said, excitedly. "They basically stepped out of their back door and off they went. This is a whole different world than I'm used to."

"Do you ski?" Blake asked.

"I love cross-country," Hayley said. "Or at least I did the few times I've done it. I don't get a lot of opportunity to get to the snow."

"There are good trails in this area," Blake told her. "Blacktail, on the northwest side of the lake is one. You should go while you're here if you have time. Garrett Starr rents skis at his Outdoor Adventures store in town."

"I might do that," she said. "But it's not much fun on your own."

The matter-of-fact way she spoke didn't sound as if she was fishing for an invitation, but he thought about asking her to go with him, anyway. Then he dismissed the idea. This was a business relationship, nothing more.

Blake slowed and turned into the circular driveway of a large, two-story log home on the opposite side of the road from the lake. "This place has no water frontage, but the house sits on two acres and has great views from the second story."

"It's huge," Hayley said as the truck stopped out front. "I can't wait to see inside. Will you do an open house, or is it view-by-appointment only?"

Blake got down from the truck and fished in his pocket for a ring of keys. "We have an open house planned for the coming weekend. Frankly, it's a godsend for you to do the staging."

"My first job after I graduated from college was as a stager's assistant. It'll be fun." Hayley joined him on the flagstone path that had been swept clean of accumulated snow, and they climbed the steps to the front door. Blake unlocked it and pushed it open. Hayley stepped inside a spacious foyer and breathed in deeply. "It smells like the forest."

"This is western red cedar," Blake said. "One of the best woods in terms of pest and disease resistance."

She walked into the living room where a river-rock chimney rose to the vaulted ceiling at the peak of the roof. "Very impressive."

"Thanks, I was pleased with this one," Blake said.

"Do you design these homes?" she asked.

He nodded. "A few, like this one, we do on spec, but mostly I draw up custom plans to a buyer's specifications. Our log homes are generally someone's dream home."

"Are you an architect?" Hayley asked. "I thought Gordon said you worked in construction for him."

"I did in the beginning," he said. "Log home construction is different from your average timber or brick home. I wanted to know how they were put together to be sure my designs would work on a practical basis. Before I designed a single home, I first learned the business from the ground up. Then I went to college and got a degree in architecture."

"I wish more architects did that," she said. "Some of the houses I see are showy but impractical. One home I looked at recently didn't even have a linen closet. I can't think of a single woman I know who would be happy with that."

"If in doubt, I consult my mother," he said, one corner of his mouth turning up.

She looked at him sideways. "I'm not quite sure if you're

joking."

"I like to keep people guessing."

Hayley turned away to hide a smile. "So this house is a full scribe type of construction, right?"

"Correct," Blake said. "The frame is made of whole logs and the walls are also comprised of whole logs stacked horizontally."

"I'm actually glad now that there isn't any furniture to distract from the construction." She pulled out her phone and started snapping photos, including close-ups of the joins where the beams met the posts. "You don't mind me taking pictures, do you?"

Normally he wouldn't think twice if someone took photos, but with Coates prowling around, he was erring on the side of caution. The joins were special, something Blake had come up with himself. "Actually, I do. Some of our processes are patented."

"Oh! I didn't know this was sensitive information," Hayley said. "I always take photos. It helps me plan the interior décor. I'll delete."

Blake chewed the inside of his cheek. Being suspicious was no way to win new customers. "Ah, go ahead. Just don't post the joins on the internet."

"I wouldn't dream of it." Her fair skin flushed. "I'm fascinated by the construction, is all. Once I start researching a topic, I get right into it."

Now he felt as if he'd insulted her. "Sorry, can't be too

careful these days. Forget I said anything. Keep the photos of the rooms."

"I'll get rid of the joins." She pressed a few buttons on her phone. "All good." She gave him a stiff smile.

"Thanks." Awkward.

Hayley walked slowly around the room, getting up close to inspect the caulking between the logs. "So there's no insulation? It must cost a fortune to heat."

"Not as much as you might think," Blake said. "Log homes are very energy efficient and the fans help push the heat back down. This one has radiant in-floor heating. Some people offset the costs with solar panels."

"How long does it take to complete a home, from the time you get the go ahead, to when it's ready to move in?" Hayley asked as they moved out of the living room and through the dining room.

"Depends on the house, but generally one to four months," Blake said. "Factors include how big it is, what kind of site preparation is needed, whether it's full scribe, timber frame, or post and beam."

"I know you told me the main types of log homes, and I did some additional reading," Hayley said. "Can you tell me more about the differences between them so I'm sure I understand?"

"Full scribe, like this one, is what people usually think of when they think of a traditional log house," Blake said. "It's so solid it can withstand anything—hurricanes, earthquakes, you name it. Downsides are they require some adjustment during the settling period, but that's something we can help with. Also, electrical wiring and plumbing need special procedures, but again those are well established."

"And post and beam?" Hayley asked as they continued down a hallway to the spacious kitchen and family room looking onto the backyard.

"It's our most popular option," Blake said. "You still have the look of whole logs in the frame of the house and as accent features. But the interior can be finished in drywall, allowing a mixture of traditional and modern elements. The method is more flexible with regard to design and less expensive than full scribe."

"That sounds like it has more interior design potential," Hayley said. "Are you able to show me one of those?"

He hesitated. They were building a post and beam house in Billings but that was half a state away. Or he could show her the one he'd built for himself. It was almost finished, but it wasn't for sale, so what was the point? He wasn't sure why he was so reluctant. It was only a house. Except that it meant so much more to him than simply a house. It was how he'd reconstructed his life after Hurricane Carrie had blown through town and flattened him.

"We have one under construction in Billings, but I don't suppose you want to go all the way there to look at it," he said.

"No, that's too far," she agreed and moved on. She

brushed her fingers approvingly across the marble counters and examined the fittings inside the cabinets. "Nice cabinetry work."

"We subcontract to a master cabinetmaker who does all our homes," Blake said. "Everything is first class."

"I can see that," she said. "What about the third building option?"

"Timber frame or hybrid," Blake said. "The logs are cut square so it looks less like a log home, more like paneling. It's similar to post and beam in that the interior can be finished in drywall and conventional wiring and plumbing are used. You have all the warmth of wood with maximum flexibility."

He led the way upstairs and stood in the hall while Hayley prowled through the bedrooms, examining everything, asking questions, listening attentively and coming back with intelligent observations or more questions.

"We can go see a hybrid house under construction, if you want," Blake said when she was done.

They returned to his truck and headed back toward Sweetheart. On the outskirts of town, situated on the lake shore, Blake slowed in front of a house under construction. Tradesmen's trucks were parked in the driveway, and the sound of hammering and the whine of a power saw could be heard from outside.

Blake walked into the open front door. "We're building this for a family from San Francisco. It's not finished, but you can easily see the difference between this and the full scribe house."

In the great room to the right, workmen were laying down a hardwood floor. Painters were spreading drop cloths in the kitchen/family room in preparation for painting the drywall. Blake stopped to talk to the supervisor while Hayley peeked into a powder room off the hallway. They made a quick tour of the upstairs, where more painters were putting a coat of white paint on the walls and trim.

"It's more like a regular house but with some feature logs," Hayley said when they'd emerged back onto the front porch. She walked a few steps on the footpath and turned to look back at it. "The full scribe feels much more solid," Hayley said. "Like a house that Papa Bear would live in."

Blake chuckled. "That fits."

"This one is solid, too, of course, but it's more like, I don't know…" She waved a hand, searching for an appropriate description. "Baby Bear's house. It's less substantial, somehow."

"Never mind that it's going to be a massive two-story structure," Blake agreed, amused. "Using your analogy, the post and beam would be Mama Bear's house."

Hayley smiled, shamefaced. "I get carried away sometimes."

"Better than the three little pigs' houses," he said. "The big bad wolf blew two out of three of them down."

"They should have built a log house," she said.

Blake had to agree.

They got back in the truck and continued back to town via Finley Road. Blake pointed out Gordon's house, a rambling single-story log home on the waterfront with a tall blue spruce tree in the front yard. "It's post and beam, but it's forty years old. He doesn't show people through it."

"I wouldn't expect him to." Hayley craned her neck to look back at the house after they passed, taking note of the location.

Farther along, Blake indicated the Starr home next to the cherry orchards. "That's a full scribe home, another of the first Gordon built. That was before I joined the company."

"Starr Orchards," Hayley read the sign out front. "Linda Starr's market stall is where I ran into Brianna. They got talking and before I knew it, Linda had invited me to their party tonight."

"You should go, their Christmas parties are legendary around Sweetheart," he said. "Just keep in mind that their house is also nearly forty years old. There've been advances in installing lighting and plumbing since then."

"I'll remember." She let a beat go past. "Are you going?"

"Yes." He tried to decipher her tone. "If you're worried about not knowing anyone…" He hesitated, reminding himself again that this was a business relationship. But that didn't mean he couldn't make a friendly gesture. "Do you want to come with me?"

For a moment, he thought she would accept. Then she shook her head. "Oh, no. Thanks, I'll be okay."

He didn't press the issue. Mingled with disappointment was a touch of relief at not complicating things. He made it a point not to date clients. Not that this would be a date, per se. And technically, she wasn't the client. But still… Okay, maybe there was more disappointment than relief. Couldn't be helped.

"Will Gordon be going, do you know?" she asked.

Blake's eyebrows rose. "I'm sure he will be."

Hayley nodded as if satisfied. "Good."

That was odd. Why should she care if Gordon went? Blake would have thought she was just making conversation except for that quietly emphatic "good" in response. It was almost as though she had another, hidden agenda besides looking at log homes.

He drove in silence for a few minutes. Darn it, he had to ask. "Do you happen to know John Coates?"

"No, the name doesn't ring a bell. Should I?" She frowned, looking confused. "Oh, do you mean of Coates Construction, that other company that builds log homes?"

"That's right," he said, searching her face for telltale signs of guilt. "John is the owner and manager."

She shook her head, still looking blank. "No, never met him. Why do you want to know?"

"Never mind," he said. "It's nothing." If she was a spy, she was a good one.

Back at the office, he loaded Hayley down with more brochures on types of wood suitable to local environments.

"Hope that's not too much all at once."

"No, it's good," Hayley said. "The more information, the better."

"Here's my card." He took one from his wallet and passed it to her. "Give me a call if you have any questions."

He waited while she got her car going and waved when she tooted her horn in farewell. Her tires spun a little on a patch of ice and threatened to swerve into a snowbank, but she deftly straightened the wheels and continued on. When she'd safely navigated onto the main road, he headed inside to the office.

Seated at his desk with a pile of folders to go through, his thoughts turned again to Hayley. Papa Bear's house. Smiling, he reached for the top folder. He had to admit, he was looking forward to seeing her at the Starr's. What had felt like a routine social engagement now looked as if it might be the most fun he'd had in months.

Then, seeing a note from Gordon on top of the folder asking him to pull together the company's financial statements for the last couple of years, his smile faded. Was Gordon getting serious about selling the business?

Blake slumped back in his chair. He'd always thought he would be the one to buy it off him when Gordon was ready to retire, but not for years yet. He'd been surprised and a little disappointed when Gordon hadn't pressed to find out the depth of Blake's interest in taking over the company. Surely after ten years, his boss would know that he was fully committed. Did he not have enough faith in Blake's ability to take the next step? Gordon had been generous and given him many opportunities, but maybe he felt Blake had reached his limit. He hated to think that Gordon, whom he looked up to as he would a father, might consider he wasn't up to the role of CEO. Maybe he should be thinking of moving on, even if Gordon didn't sell to John Coates. Everything inside him rejected the idea. But what was his alternative?

Straightening, he pushed aside those futile thoughts and got back to work, going into the company files to locate the financial statements Gordon wanted. When he'd emailed them on, he logged into his own bank account to check his financial standing. It only confirmed what he already knew. He'd started investing in the private company a few years ago when he'd become manager, taking shares in lieu of pay increases. Whatever dividends he earned, he plowed right back into more shares, but he had nowhere near a majority. All his savings had gone into his house on the Point. Only if he sold it could he afford to buy a majority interest in the company.

He'd bought the land years ago on a recommendation from Gordon, even though, at the time, building a home of his own hadn't been on Blake's radar. The lot had sat idle until Carrie left two years ago. Needing something to keep himself from going crazy, he'd decided to build himself a house. At first, it was just to have something to occupy himself, but as it began to take shape, the house started to mean more and more to him. He'd designed it and built it largely with his own hands. The house was his dream home, achieved after years of hard work. His mother had never owned her own home, and she still rented. To Blake, home ownership, especially a home as unique as his, was the sweet smell of success and personal achievement. Despite all the odds, he'd made something of himself. To have to sell it would feel like an admission of failure, that he couldn't quite cut it in the world he'd aspired to.

Shadows grew across the yard outside his window and onto the factory roof. On the other hand, leading this company was also something he aspired to. Blake sighed and shut his laptop. There were no easy answers.

"Come on, Rebel. Let's take a walk."

Chapter Six

Tuesday evening, December 17

F OR THE STARR'S Christmas party, Hayley took Brianna's advice and pulled on skinny jeans, a thick cream-colored pullover, and knee-high boots. At five p.m., it was already dark, and a few light flakes of snow were falling. She thought worriedly about the chains she hadn't gotten around to getting. But, according to the weather forecast, the snow wasn't supposed to amount to more than an inch or two. Hopefully, the snowplows would be out.

She drove down Finley Road, keeping watch for the orchard sign out front. The Starr house was easily identified without it. All the windows of the house glowed with light, and the roof and sides of the huge log home were outlined with colored lights. The large circular driveway was packed with trucks and cars. In the side yard, a group of people stood around a blazing brazier. Flames and sparks leaped into the dark sky.

She parked and got out of her car. The sound of bells made her turn. Across the lane, through the rows of bare-limbed cherry trees, an open sleigh went by, pulled by a massive Clydesdale with a golden coat and a blonde mane and tail. The passengers were muffled to their ears with scarves and hats. The romantic scene could have come straight out of a storybook.

Hayley watched the sleigh until it turned into a yard in front of a shed a few hundred yards away. Then she ran up the steps of the house, excited about the prospect of seeing Gordon and Brianna again and meeting her aunt for the first time. On the massive wood slab door, below a wreath of cedar boughs and pine cones, a handwritten sign read, "Welcome. Please come in."

She turned the handle and entered a large foyer where a staircase led to the second story. The scent of pine and cedar from the numerous Christmas wreaths and candles mingled with the aroma of hot appetizers laid out on the oak table in the dining room to her right along with cheese platters, cold appetizers, and baked Christmas goodies. The heady scent of mulled cherry wine permeated the cozy atmosphere.

Judging by the sounds of female laughter and clanking pans coming from the back of the house, that way lay the kitchen. She turned instead to the living room on her left, where people mingled, standing or seated, amid a buzz of conversation and laughter.

Blake stood in a cluster of guests, his broad back to the mantelpiece. Seeing her, he smiled, and her heart leaped. She hadn't realized how much she'd been looking forward to seeing him again until this moment. From his vantage point, he had a view of the entry. Had he been watching for her arrival?

He excused himself from the people he was with and came toward her. "I wasn't sure you would come."

"I feel like an interloper, but I wouldn't have missed it," she said.

"Don't feel as if you're intruding. The Starrs are very hospitable." He touched her arm. "Let's get you a drink. There's mulled wine in the dining room and regular wine or beer in the kitchen. Robert brought out his best scotch for the occasion."

"The mulled wine is awesome," she said, moving into the dining room. "I'd love some of that."

Blake poured some for her into a Russian tea glass. "Come, I'll introduce you to people."

Together they made the rounds. Hayley said hello to Linda and thanked her again for the invitation. Linda, in turn, introduced her to her husband Robert, and she met three of the Starr brothers—Adam, Garrett and Cody—all tall, handsome men. With the exception of Garrett, who she learned was single, they were accompanied by their wives and small children or babies.

After chatting with the Starrs for a few minutes, Hayley turned to Blake. "Is Gordon here? I'd like to say hello."

"He's here somewhere." Glancing around, Blake nodded to indicate a woman with shoulder-length silver hair wearing a red dress dotted with tiny springs of holly. "That's Anita, his wife."

Anita was engaged in a lively discussion with another woman. Hayley didn't want to interrupt, but she resolved to find an excuse to chat with her aunt, too, before the evening was over.

A tall woman with long curling blonde hair, who looked to be about six months pregnant, came by with a plate of skewers of satay beef. "Hi, I'm Kelly. Help yourself. These just came off the grill."

"I'm Hayley." She took one and a napkin. "Thanks. You're married to...one of the brothers, I can't remember which."

"Cody." Kelly nodded to the athletic, dark-haired man with his hand resting on a small blond boy's shoulder. "That's our son, Ricky." She tilted her head on one side. "Are you new in town?"

"I'm here looking at log homes," Hayley said.

"Oh, you should talk to Blake or Gordon."

"I am. Blake showed me a couple of their houses." Hayley glanced around for him, but he'd gotten separated from her by the ebb and flow of guests. More people were arriving all the time. The volume of conversation had risen. She finally spotted him talking to an older man with gray hair and chiseled features, who bore a family resemblance to Robert and his sons. He must be the patriarch, Nathan Starr.

Next, Hayley chatted with Emma, Adam's wife, who carried a toddler on her hip and talked about her work with sustainable crops. Then Emma moved off. Kelly was surrounded by a knot of young people in search of appetizers. One of them was a fellow named Angus. Between bites he told her he worked for Gordon in the factory measuring, cutting, and notching the logs in preparation for assembling the houses.

"I toured two of the homes today," she said. Eager to learn more about her uncle, she asked, "Do you enjoy the work? Is Mr. Renton a good boss?"

"He's great," Angus said promptly. "Pays well, doesn't quibble about overtime, and always gives a bonus at this time of year, whether sales are good or not."

"Are sales not always good?" Hayley was pleased to hear of her uncle's generosity. So far, everyone she'd met had nothing but good things to say about him. She still couldn't fathom what her sweet, loving mother could have done to her older brother to make Gordon angry enough to cut her out of his life, but she had to find out and somehow fix it.

"Some years are better than others," Angus admitted, in between bites of a cocktail frank. "Last year, profits were down 10 percent. I'm taking business classes at night school, so I'm interested in this stuff. Blake's going to bring in a new machine for stripping the bark off the logs, so efficiency should improve next year. Blake is always looking for ways to increase productivity—"

"Do I hear someone taking my name in vain?" Blake

came up between Hayley and Angus.

"Hey, Mr. Dennison." Angus shifted his feet, looking embarrassed at being overheard talking about his manager. "I was just telling, um—"

"Hayley," she supplied. "He was saying how well the company was doing."

Angus shot her a glance, eyebrows raised, but didn't say anything.

Blake clapped a hand on Angus's shoulder. "No shop talk, okay?" he said easily. "We're here to have fun."

"Sure. Excuse me, I need another one of those beef things." He nodded at Hayley. "Nice to meet you." Then he moved away, leaving her alone with Blake.

"What's the deal?" Hayley adopted a teasing tone to cover her discomfort at being caught pumping Angus for information about her uncle. "Aren't employees allowed to talk about the company? What are you hiding?"

"Nothing." Blake's eyes held hers steadily. "What are you trying to find out?"

"I'm just curious." Awareness buzzed between them, a fizzing chemistry made complicated by a touch of guilt on her part and suspicion on his. At least that's what his close scrutiny appeared to be. Had he already figured out who she was? Was he shielding his boss from an unwanted relative? Or was it something else entirely? Maybe the company was in more serious trouble than Angus knew and Blake didn't want to scare off a potential client.

"Seriously, is everything okay at Sweetheart Log Homes?" she asked. If Gordon's business was in trouble, she knew her mom would want to help if she could.

"Understandably, your client wouldn't be happy if she ordered a home and the company went belly-up before it was finished," Blake said smoothly. "But there are no problems with the company. It's business as usual."

"That's good to know." From the corner of her eye, she glimpsed her uncle enter the room. "There's Gordon now."

Blake put a warning hand on her forearm. "I wasn't joking when I asked Angus not to talk shop. Gordon is tired and stressed. His downtime is important for him to relax."

"I was only going to say hello," Hayley assured him. "I don't know many people here. And it seems polite."

"Of course," he said, releasing her. "I'm sure he'll be glad to see you."

"You're very protective of him." A beat went by while she studied Blake's unreadable expression. Another terrible thought occurred to her, unrelated to business. "He doesn't have an illness, does he?"

Blake shook his head sharply. "Gordon's in the best of health. Why would you think he was ill?"

"No reason," she said. "It's just that you seem to put up barriers around him. And you say he's tired and stressed."

"If he's tired and stressed, it's because he works too hard. He's always the first one in the office and often the last to leave." Blake passed his glass to his other hand and flexed his fingers. It was done casually, but Hayley noticed. Blake seemed a little stressed too. "If I'm protective it's because he's been like a father to me," Blake went on. "Gordon showed faith in me when a lot of others didn't and gave me opportunities when no one else would."

"Have you known him a long time?" Hayley asked.

Blake nodded. "I was friends with Garrett Starr when we were young; although in high school we drifted apart. I was in danger of getting in with a bad crowd. Gordon's wife is friends with my mom and with Linda Starr. Anita could see what was happening and put a word in Gordon's ear. He gave me a job and mentored me. I can honestly say he turned my life around."

"Don't forget Anita's input," Hayley said.

"Yes, she's wonderful too," Blake agreed. "And also, thanks to their intervention, Garrett and I renewed our friendship."

"You two look deep in conversation," Gordon said, appearing at their side with a glass of scotch in hand. He'd shed his work uniform of pale blue shirt and navy pants for a houndstooth vest over a plaid shirt.

"Hi." Now Hayley knew where Brianna got her dress sense, she noted with amusement. "Blake was just telling me how you gave him his start."

"I needed a factory hand, so I put him to work." Gordon's eyes twinkled behind his rimless glasses.

"And helped me through college," Blake said.

"Ah, but I had an ulterior motive." Gordon addressed his next words to Hayley. "I could see he was smart, as well as strong, could work with his hands, and he had leadership potential. I wanted to get the most out of him."

"Brains and brawn." Hayley gave Blake an admiring glance that was only partly mocking. "The whole package."

"Enough." Blake grimaced. "You two are embarrassing me."

Gordon laughed. He seemed relaxed tonight, Hayley thought, but she didn't know him that well. Maybe those lines around his mouth and eyes weren't normally so deep.

"What did you think of the spec house?" Gordon asked Hayley, changing the subject.

"I was very impressed," she said. "I wish I could see a post and beam to compare."

"Oh, but—" Gordon gave Blake a questioning glance.

Blake was staring fixedly into his drink.

Sensing an undercurrent, Hayley waited to see if he would say anything. He didn't speak, so she went on. "I was checking real estate in the area and noticed that Coates Construction has a post and beam for sale in Polson. I'll view it tomorrow, if I can get an appointment."

"We don't want her going to the competition," Gordon said, gently chiding Blake.

Blake cleared his throat, looking uncomfortable. "I could show you a post and beam house. Not the one in Billings; this is on Finley Point. It's not for sale though."

"It's the best house you've ever done." Gordon regarded Blake with paternal pride and something else that Hayley couldn't decipher. Sadness? Worry?

Hayley was confused. Earlier, Blake had denied having a post and beam house to view nearby. Why didn't he want to show it to her? "I'd love to see it, if it's no trouble."

"Sure, no problem." Blake gave her a thin smile. "We could do that tomorrow, if you like."

"Thanks." Hayley turned to Gordon with a playful tone. "And that's all I'm going to say about log houses tonight. I shouldn't be bothering you with business talk at a party."

"I don't mind," Gordon said jovially. "I can talk logs all day long."

"And into the night," his wife said dryly, joining them. She put an affectionate arm around her husband's waist. She smiled at Hayley. "Hi, I'm Anita. I hear you're from California. Were you anywhere near the wildfires?"

"Not me, but my mom just missed having to be evacuated." Hayley shut her mouth to stop herself from blurting out the truth, right here, right now, and letting the chips fall where they may. If it was only her feelings to take into account, she would. But her mom was too important to risk an adverse reaction from her brother. Nor was it fair to blindside Gordon at a party, surrounded by people. Especially if he was already stressed about something.

"That must have been terrifying," Anita said. "I hope she's all right."

"She's fine. Although she's thinking of moving out of the area," Hayley said. "Maybe even to the mountains." She could so picture her mom living in Sweetheart, in a log home built by her brother. And coming to parties like this one, enjoying festivities with her extended family.

Brianna and Angus, both with red cheeks and snowflakes clinging to their hats, came through the front door, laughing. Angus shot a glance at Gordon and disappeared down the hall to the kitchen. Brianna stamped the snow off her boots and unwound her long scarf.

"Blake, Hayley, you've got to go on the sleigh ride," she said, striding over, her cheeks pink and eyes sparkling. "It's awesome."

"I've never been on a horse-drawn sleigh," Hayley said. "It looks fun."

"Go on," Brianna said. "But hurry. Will is calling for last passengers before he returns Bessie to the neighbors."

"How about it?" Hayley said to Blake. "Are you up for a sleigh ride?"

"Sure, let's go," Blake said.

"Why don't you go again, too, Brianna?" Gordon urged his daughter. "There's room for three, isn't there?"

"Four," Brianna said, uncertainly. "But I just got back from a ride."

"Oh, go on," Gordon encouraged. "How often do you get out on the sleigh?"

Brianna wrinkled her nose as if to say, *Da-a-d.*

"Don't make an issue of it, Gord," Anita murmured.

"Of course you're welcome to join us, Brianna," Blake said.

"That would be awesome," Hayley added, meaning it.

"Nope, I'm feeling chilled," Brianna said firmly. "I'm going to get a glass of mulled wine and go stand by the fire. But you guys enjoy. Catch you later." With a little wave, she wove through the guests toward the dining room.

"The lady knows her own mind," Blake said. "Excuse us," he added to Gordon and Anita.

"Nice to meet you," Hayley said to Anita and smiled at Gordon before following Blake. When she reached the foyer, she glanced over her shoulder to see Gordon and Anita in a close huddle, talking earnestly.

"What was that all about?" Hayley asked, taking her coat down from the rack. "Gordon didn't look happy that we're going without Brianna."

"Don't worry about it." Blake shoved his feet into his boots.

"Maybe I should head back to the hotel," Hayley said, still concerned that she'd put a foot wrong somehow. "You've put yourself out enough for me for one day."

"I was only doing my job earlier and, anyway, it's no hardship," Blake assured her. "I want to go on the sleigh. I could use some fresh air. It was getting stuffy in there."

Still, she hesitated. She didn't want to upset her uncle.

"Seriously, it's fine," Blake said, opening the front door

for her.

Their boots crunched on the crisp dry snow as they walked toward the colored Christmas lights outlining the roof of the large building, which Blake told her was the cherry-packing shed. The track was uneven, a mixture of snow and frozen mud. Hayley had to pick her way carefully. Halfway between the house and the shed, where it was darkest, Hayley stumbled, and Blake put out a hand to steady her.

Instead of walking on, he stopped. "Back there? Gordon has this idea that Brianna and I are going to get together."

"I see." Hayley felt a stab of disappointment. Suddenly, the pair's easy familiarity with each other appeared to her in a completely different light. In a way, it made so much sense. Then she thought about his words more carefully. "What are you saying? *Are* you and Brianna a couple?"

"No," Blake said. "Gordon's got it all wrong."

"Okay." She tried to read his face, but the light was too dim.

"Hey, are you guys coming?" the man waiting with the horse and sleigh outside the shed called.

Hayley had more questions, but they would have to wait.

"Hayley, this is Will Starr. Will, Hayley," Blake said as they approached. "Have you got time for one more ride?"

Will's cheeks were as red as the Santa hat perched at a jaunty angle on his fair hair. The horse's damp golden coat steamed in the frosty air. "Of course. Hello, Hayley," Will said. "Hop aboard."

Blake took her gloved hand and helped her climb up the buckboard. She settled on the cushioned bench seat, and Blake sat beside her. Then he pulled the thick fake fur throw over their laps.

"Warm enough?" he asked. His thigh pressed alongside hers, and their arms touched all the way from shoulder to elbow. When he turned to speak to her, she could feel the warmth of his breath on her cheek.

She nodded. She didn't know whether it was the excitement of the sleigh ride or Blake sitting so close, but her heart was thumping.

"No one else coming?" Will asked, climbing up front. He picked up the reins and whip.

"Doesn't appear so." Blake glanced down the lane leading to the house, but it was empty.

"Then we're off. Gee up, Bessie." Will inserted earbuds into his ears and his head moved in time to music only he could hear. He slapped the long reins over the horse's rump, and they set off at a slow trot down the lane and into the orchard.

Once away from the lights of the shed and the house, deep in the orchard, Hayley looked up between the snow-covered branches of the trees to a clear night sky thickly strewn with stars. The bells on the harness jingled softly, and the runners made a soft susurration as they glided over the hard-packed snow.

"I've never seen so many stars in my whole life," Hayley whispered, awestruck.

"I never get tired of the Montana sky." Blake's voice was hushed too. "Day or night, it's beautiful."

"There's a shooting star!" Hayley clutched his arm. "Did you see it?"

"Now you have to make a wish."

She tore her gaze away from his face and tried to come up with a wish, but all she could think of was the man beside her, so close she could feel his warmth beneath the fur blanket.

"Are you okay?" he asked.

"Fine," she said, massaging her neck. "I was getting a crick in my neck from looking up at the stars."

"What about your wish?"

"Okay, here goes." She shut her eyes and crossed her fingers on both hands. *I wish Blake would kiss me.* As soon as she thought it, she took it back. That was a stupid wish. Opening her eyes again, she turned to Blake. "How many wishes do I get?"

"One per shooting star."

"Well, I'm going to tack on another. It was a huge star, after all."

I wish I could find the right moment to tell my uncle about Mom and that he would be happy to have found her again.

A happy daydream ran through her head of her mother coming to Sweetheart for Christmas and them both spending the holiday with Gordon and his family. Maybe her mom would love the town so much she would decide to move here.

"You're not still making wishes, are you?" Blake said, sounding amused. "If you ask for too much, the universe gets cranky and doesn't grant anything."

"Now you tell me!" Hayley gave a faux sigh. "None of it will probably come true anyway."

"Aren't you going to tell me what you wished for?" Blake teased.

"No." She gave his arm a gentle shove. "That's a surefire way to ensure the wish won't come true."

"I thought maybe you were wishing you were buying a house out here instead of your client." His voice was warm now and sincere.

"Not even close." But it wasn't such a terrible thought.

The sleigh emerged from the trees, and the lane curved around with the orchard on their right and an open, snow-covered field to their left. In the distance, the mountains rose black and silent in the crystalline air.

Hayley leaned back and drank in the night. "I think I could actually live here though."

"Really? You already like Montana that much?"

"Well, I'd hate to live so far from my mother and brother, but, yes."

The sleigh blades swished softly in the snow, and the bells on the harness jingled. Blake's dark eyes smiled down at her, his expression thoughtful. Hayley could hardly breathe. It was actually going to happen. He was going to kiss her. His mouth, warm and mobile, was so close, all she had to do was lift her face, and their lips would touch. He wanted it, she could tell. All of her yearned to close that gap.

Oh, but how could she kiss him, when she wasn't being up-front with him about why she was in Sweetheart? It wasn't right, or fair to him.

Turning away was one of the hardest things she'd ever done. A cool waft of air came between them. When she opened her eyes, he'd drawn away, too, a slight frown creasing his eyebrows. Embarrassment heated her cheeks. She'd been swept up in the romance of the sleigh ride, in the chemistry that danced between them, the moon and the mountains and the man. Forgetting, for a few magical moments, that she was here under false pretenses and that he was going to be rightfully annoyed when he found out the truth.

Will turned the horse down the lane toward the cherry-packing shed. Suddenly, Hayley couldn't wait to get out of the sleigh. A few minutes later, Blake helped her down from the sleigh, and she stepped gingerly onto the icy ground.

"Okay?" he asked, as she found her footing.

"Yes, thank you." His solicitous query made her feel even worse. Her cover story had mushroomed out of control, and the fact that she was still using it bothered her—a lot. Blake was a nice guy, and it wasn't right to lead him on.

Her mom's card was in her purse. The minute she got inside, she would corner Gordon and give it to him. She knew enough about her uncle now to know he was a decent man, a family man, well-liked by everyone. All she could do was tell him his sister cared about him and wanted to make contact. He would either talk to Joyce and work things out, or he wouldn't.

As she and Blake walked back to the party, she filled the awkward silence with questions about cherry picking and orchards, which he answered as best he could.

Once inside, Hayley turned to Blake. "Thanks, that was wonderful. I'm just going to go…." She gestured vaguely.

"Sure." His gaze was impassive. "Talk to you later."

With a sense of relief and regret at leaving him, she wove her way through the mingling guests in the living room in search of Gordon. She couldn't see him anywhere. Nor was he with the crowd around the dining table filling small plates with appetizers. Next, she headed down the hall to the kitchen, hoping to find him having a glass of scotch with Robert, but a quick scan of the room was all it took for her heart to sink. The backyard brazier then. Outside on the covered patio, she stood shivering, while her desperate gaze moved from glowing face to glowing face. Gordon wasn't there. That's when she realized she hadn't seen Anita, either.

She turned to go back inside and bumped into Brianna coming out of the kitchen wearing her jacket. "Have you seen your father? I wanted to speak with him a moment."

"He and Mom went home," Brianna said. "They wanted to get an early start in the morning for the drive to Marietta. They still have to pack and do a bunch of stuff before they go."

"Oh, I see." Hayley could have kicked herself for the missed opportunity; for going on a sleigh ride with Blake when she should have been talking to her uncle. How could she have allowed herself to get sidetracked? Blake, obviously. But she needed to focus. She was here for her mother, not to have a fling with a guy when whatever romance might ensue would be as brief as a shooting star.

"I'm going back out to the brazier," Brianna said. "Want to come?"

"I'll probably head back to the hotel," Hayley said. "It's been a long day."

"How was the sleigh ride?" Brianna asked.

"Beautiful." Hayley felt a bittersweet pang. "Thanks for getting me invited to the party. I'm so glad I came."

"I'm glad you did too." Brianna raised her glasses. "I'd better get out there. See you soon."

Hayley found Linda, expressed her appreciation for the invitation, and said goodbye, then went looking for Blake to make her farewells to him. He was in a corner of the dining room, talking and laughing with Garret and Cody Starr. She hesitated, rather than approach. The trio looked so close and tight-knit that she would feel awkward breaking in just to say goodbye. So she quietly got her coat and slipped out the front door.

She cast a frustrated backward glance at the lit-up house and the figures visible through the windows. The party had been fun, and she'd enjoyed meeting people, but she hadn't accomplished what she'd come for, to give the card to her uncle.

It was only six forty-five p.m. She could drop in at Gordon's house on the way back to the hotel. She turned right on Finley Road instead of left and drove the short distance to her uncle's residence. The tall blue spruce was easy to spot, and she'd made mental note of the address on the mailbox earlier. But there were no lights on inside, at least none that she could see. She pulled into the driveway and sat there, idling. They could have gone out for dinner, to visit someone else, or to do last-minute shopping for a wedding gift.

She weighed her options. She could drop the card in the mailbox and head home to California tomorrow. Gordon would at least get her mother's card, and he could decide what action he wanted to take. But everything in her rebelled against driving across three states only to leave without telling her uncle in person who she was and why she was there. Also, she'd agreed to stage the spec home and didn't like to go back on her word.

Alternatively, she could stick around, check out this other house tomorrow with Blake, and fill in the rest of the time decorating the spec home. It was only two days. Her mom had Lydia visiting for the week, and they always had a ball when they got together. Brad was still away. Her work back home was under control, with nothing that required her presence in person until the new year. She might as well stay put until her uncle got back on Friday. Nothing would put her off from talking to him then. Then she could drive home on the weekend and be back in plenty of time for Christmas.

Later, as she lay in bed and stared up at the ceiling, she thought over what had happened—or rather, hadn't happened—on the sleigh ride, and had to admit that, contrary to what she'd told Blake, she wasn't entirely okay. Something had happened out there under the glittering night sky. Like a shooting star, her feelings for him had rocketed from mild attraction to an active desire for something to happen between them. A kiss, a touch. Maybe more.

No, Blake was off-limits. Unless she could be straight with him, she couldn't pursue anything remotely resembling a romance. She'd painted herself into a corner with her story about a client in California. It wasn't at all what she'd intended, but it had happened, and now she had to see it through. Until she spoke to Gordon and gave him the card, she was stuck.

Speaking of truth telling, had Blake given her the whole story when he'd said he and Brianna weren't an item? Why would Gordon push them together unless there was a good reason? Maybe Brianna had a thing for Blake. Even if Blake didn't reciprocate Brianna's feelings, there was no way Hayley would risk upsetting her cousin.

But another plus of staying until Gordon returned in a few days was that she could learn more about log homes. She was seriously falling in love with them and couldn't wait to see another of Blake's house designs.

And, well, face it, she also couldn't wait to see Blake.

Chapter Seven

BLAKE GOT TO the office early to do some paperwork before he picked up Hayley at the hotel. He'd spent half an hour making progress on his in-tray, when he heard Brianna arrive. A moment later, the scent of freshly baked cookies drew him out of his office.

"Morning." He snagged a snowman cookie from the plate she'd placed on the edge of the reception counter and bit off the head. "These are good."

"Don't eat them all," Brianna said, batting his hand away. "I'm taking some down to the factory."

"To Angus?" he said, grinning.

"Shut up." But she broke into a goofy smile.

"Did your parents get away all right this morning?" Blake asked.

"Crack of dawn," Brianna said, yawning. "I suspect they'll be talking about whether or not to sell the company all the way to Marietta." She shrugged. "Selling might not be so bad. Dad could retire in comfort. You would likely stay on as manager. Bigger company, bigger paycheck."

"I wouldn't bank on that, not with Coates in charge," Blake said. "He would put his own man in the position."

"You don't know that for sure," Brianna said. "I wouldn't mind for myself if Dad sold. I'm only working here to help out the family. I'd rather be a full-time coder than a combination accountant, receptionist, and coffee lady."

Blake took another cookie. "Speaking of which, isn't it your turn to clean the staff kitchen?"

Brianna whisked the plate off the counter and put it on her desk, out of reach. "It's your turn. I did it last week."

"Later," he said. "I'm taking Hayley out to see the house on Finley Point."

Brianna's eyes widened. "Your house? You're surely not putting that on the market."

"No, never," he said. "But it's the only post and beam we've got that she can look at. We don't want her going to Coates."

"Heaven forbid. Did she enjoy the sleigh ride?"

He thought of Hayley's face beneath her fur-trimmed hat, gazing dreamily up at the star-strewn sky, her eyes huge in the starlight. "It was a nice clear night."

"Pfft," Brianna said. "Did you kiss her?"

Blake had spent a good portion of last night wondering just what her lips would have felt like beneath his—if she hadn't turned aside. He'd gotten the impression she was attracted right up until the last second. So, yeah, not finding out had been disappointing. Maybe he'd been wrong about her being attracted to him, or maybe she thought a kiss would be inappropriate. "No, and I'm not going to. She's a client."

"Not exactly," Brianna argued. "Her client is our potential client. And now she's doing a job for us. We're more like colleagues. You could totally go after her. I can tell you like her."

"She's okay," he said, his nonchalance not very convincing.

"I might invite her for a girls' night out," Brianna said.

"You've gotten very friendly with her awfully quickly," Blake said.

"She's nice; I like her." Brianna sent him a sidelong glance. "Anyway, who went on a romantic sleigh ride with her, hmm?"

"Romantic? No way. It was a business sleigh ride." As soon as he said it he knew how ridiculous it sounded.

Brianna laughed out loud. "Tell that to the judge. Or, rather, tell it to my dad." Then she sobered. "I'm sorry about that weirdness on Saturday night. Could he have been any more obvious about trying to throw me at you?"

"Don't worry about it. You and I both know the score. Someday you'll bring some poor schmuck home, and your father will forget he even harbored this notion of you and me."

"I wouldn't go out with a schmuck," she said indignantly.

"No, Angus is cool," Blake said. "Why are you keeping him a secret?"

"What makes you think it's Angus?"

"Come on, I saw you two at the Starr's."

Brianna gave an exasperated sigh. "He works in the factory. Dad thinks I could do better."

"That doesn't make sense," Blake said. "I started in the factory. Your dad thinks I'm okay."

She snorted. "Dad think the sun shines out of your 'you know what.'"

Blake changed the subject. "Is it just me, or do you think it's a bit odd that Hayley's staging our spec home? Her client hasn't even bought a house yet. If she ever will." He hadn't intended to bring this up with Brianna, but he trusted her judgment.

"No, I think she's excited about log homes and likes a challenge," Brianna said. "Anyway, I'm not looking a gift horse in the mouth. I'm going to pick her brains as much as I can. Myra was okay, but her décor was a little bland and cookie-cutter."

"Well, yeah." Blake had to agree. "I would love to see what a professional interior designer could do with one of our houses. I just don't know why Hayley wants to be bothered. She came here for her client, not looking for extra work to take on."

"She likes it here in Sweetheart," Brianna said. "She's not

in any hurry to leave."

"No, she's not, is she?" Blake said. "Again, doesn't that strike you as strange?"

"Not necessarily." Brianna shrugged. "Maybe she's taking some personal time as well."

"She's certainly made friends quickly," Blake mused. "Invited to the Starr's party, going around the market with you, and now you're going to ask her to go out on the town with you."

As he had almost asked her to go skiing with him.

"She's fun. Come on, it's not like that's never happened to any other visitors before," Brianna said. "We're a friendly bunch in Sweetheart."

Blake hesitated, then lowered his voice. "What if she's not who she seems?"

Brianna blinked. "What are you suggesting?"

"Is it a coincidence that we're getting all this interest from Coates just as she shows up in town?" Blake said. "We're reluctant to talk to him because we see him as a hostile figure, and yet we're opening our homes to Hayley and showing her through all our houses."

"The houses aren't a secret," Brianna said, laughing. "We want people to look through them. We're in the business of selling them."

"Yeah, but the other day she was taking a ton of photos, including close-ups of the joins in the logs."

"So she's thorough. You, of all people, should understand and appreciate that attention to detail." Brianna shrugged. "Anyway, if she was working for Coates, she wouldn't talk about going to look at his houses."

"Unless she was only pretending to look at them as part of her cover. I know it seems far-fetched but..." He shrugged. "I don't want to find out differently the hard way."

"I think you're way off base," Brianna said. "She's too open and honest."

"Okay, then, why did Hayley ask your father about his family and his childhood?"

"She's just humoring him," Brianna said. "He loves talking about that stuff."

"Does he?" Blake said. "He talks about traveling around when he was young, and his early days in Sweetheart, but I've never heard him mention where he grew up or things that happened when he was a kid. Or his sister. I've only heard about her from your mother. Now I gather they're estranged."

"Now that you mention it, I didn't even know he had a sister until a couple of years ago when Mom told me," Brianna said. "I knew he grew up in California somewhere as a foster kid, but I assume he doesn't talk about his family because his childhood wasn't particularly happy. I don't see Hayley asking about his background as anything sinister."

"Unless she's lulling him into regarding her as a friend and confident," Blake suggested. "He gets to trust her and starts divulging more and more information. Pretty soon, she could ask him anything about the company, and he would tell her."

"Geez, Louise, when did you become so suspicious?" Brianna said. "You're the one always saying we should give people the benefit of the doubt. Don't judge a book by its cover, yada yada."

"I do think that," Blake said. "But there's something about Hayley…"

"What?" Brianna demanded. "How nice she is?"

"She is nice," he had to agree. And beautiful, sweet, kind, and seemingly genuinely interested in people. But there was something about her that Blake found hard to put into words. He just had a feeling that she was hiding something about herself that would cause them to view her completely differently if they knew the truth.

"She seems too good to be true," he said at last, aware his conclusion sounded lame.

"Ah, I know what you're doing," Brianna said suddenly. "You're looking for reasons not to like her."

"Don't be silly," he said. "Why would I do that?"

"Because you're scared," Brianna said. "You've finally met someone you really like and are attracted to, someone who could make you forget how Carrie hurt you. And then you'd have no excuse to be alone anymore."

"Don't be ridiculous. I've known Hayley for five minutes," Blake blustered. "Anyway, that's crazy. Why would I want to be alone?"

Brianna gave him a shrewd glance. "You tell me, because I sure don't understand it. But that's what you've been doing for the past two years, guarding your single status like it was a prize."

He looked at his watch, then leaned over the counter and grabbed another cookie. Wrapping it in a paper napkin he stuffed it in his pocket. "I've got to hit the road." He reached for his jacket. Rebel got off his mat by the woodstove and padded to the door. "Hayley's waiting."

HAYLEY WAS UP early that morning for breakfast in the hotel dining room. Back in her room, she got out her laptop and spent an hour or so working on a proposal to do the interior design of a boutique hotel on the Big Sur coast. She was almost ready to call it quits and go meet Blake when her mother called. "Hi, Mom. How are you doing?"

"I'm fine, honey," Joyce said. "Do you know yet when you'll be back? Lydia's present to us this year is tickets to see Andrea Bocelli on Saturday. Will you be able to make it, or should we give your ticket to someone else?"

"I'd love to see Lydia—and Andrea Bocelli—but I'll be here another few days at least," Hayley said. "How long is she staying?"

"Just until Sunday," Joyce said.

It was roughly a twenty-hour drive from Sweetheart to Fallbrook, not taking into account breaks along the way and possible weather delays. Even if she drove all day Friday and Saturday, she still might not make it.

"I'm sorry, you'd better see if someone else can go," Hayley said. "Give Lydia my love and tell her thanks for thinking of me. I'll write to her soon." She paused. "Have you heard from Brad?"

"He called yesterday," her mother said. "They're still trying to get supplies to people on remote islands. He doesn't think he'll make it back in time for Christmas."

"Oh, that's too bad," Hayley said. "We'll miss him." It wouldn't be the first Christmas that Brad had been somewhere else. She ought to be used to his absence at key family events but it only got more frustrating as the years went by.

"Hayley?" her mom began cautiously. "Are you really there on business or is there…some other reason?"

"Pardon?" Hayley was suddenly on alert. "What other reason could there be?"

"A man?"

Hayley's thoughts flew to Blake. Nervous laughter bubbled up. "No."

"I've never known you to go away on a business for more than a day or two," Joyce persisted. "Usually you talk to me about your new projects, but this time you didn't say a word about who it was for or what you were doing."

"Well…" Hayley put an arm around her stomach. She

and her mom were close, and she hated that she wasn't being open with her. "This project is tricky. I'm not sure if I'm going to be successful. I didn't want to talk about it too much and jinx myself."

"So it's not a man?" Joyce pried gently. "It's okay, you don't have to tell me unless you want to."

"There's nothing to tell." Hayley tugged on a strand of hair. That wasn't true, and she was dying to talk about Blake. "Okay, there is a guy. He's cute and nice, and I like him." *A lot.* "I just met him, though, and I'll be saying goodbye as soon as I'm finished here. Nothing is going to happen."

"How do you know that?" Joyce said reasonably. "Does he like you?"

He'd almost kissed her. The memory of how close she'd come to touching her lips to his tormented her.

"I think so, but, as I said, it probably won't go anywhere," Hayley said. "I'm a potential customer, and he's a bit reserved." By which she meant he seemed suspicious of her. Which she deserved, but until her uncle came back, she couldn't explain. Restless, Hayley carried her empty coffee cup over to the hospitality tray.

"Hayley, you have a tendency to overthink things. Jump in, make the first move," Joyce advised. "You'll know soon enough how he feels."

"That's not going to work in this case," she said. "It's…complicated. I have other priorities." God that sounded so lame, so false.

"You're being awfully mysterious," Joyce said.

Hayley groaned inwardly. She couldn't continue to hide the true purpose of her trip from her mother. "There's something I need to tell you. I'm not here on business."

There was a sharp intake of breath on the other end of the line. "I knew it. Whatever it is, you can tell me, honey," her mom said in a quiet voice, as if Hayley was about to give her bad news. "Are you in trouble?"

"What? No!" Her laughter broke the tension. This illustrated exactly why she had to come clean. If she didn't, her mother would conjure up the worst possible scenario and worry herself sick. "The town I'm in is called Sweetheart. It's on Flathead Lake in northwestern Montana. It's so beautiful with the mountains and the water..." Hayley trailed off, aware she was stalling. "Anyway, I came here because—are you sitting down?" Hayley took a deep breath. "I found your brother, Gordon."

There was a long silence on the other end of the line.

"Mom? Are you there?"

"Go on," Joyce said, sounding hopeful and terrified at the same time.

"He has a company that builds log homes. Oh, Mom, you should see these houses, they're amazing. His wife's name is Anita, and he has three grown children: Daniel, Aiden and Brianna."

"Oh, my." Joyce's voice quavered. "Tell me more. Tell

me everything."

But there was no way she could tell her mother every-thing, like that Gordon had refused to acknowledge Joyce. Oh, why had she opened her mouth? There was no possibil-ity now of quietly leaving town and pretending this whole episode never took place. Now she absolutely had to get her uncle to agree to talk to her mom.

"I haven't had a chance to tell him who I am yet," Hay-ley said. "It's going to be a shock, and I want to do it at the optimum time. He's so busy that it's hard to get him alone. And now he's gone away for a couple of days. But, Mom, he's been so nice to me. He's really a great guy."

A watery sniff on the other end of the line made her real-ize her mother was crying. "When he gets back to town, I'm going to talk to him," Hayley went on. "I have your Christ-mas card to give to him."

"Oh, Hayley." The pain in Joyce's voice was evident. "You're putting him on the spot. It would have been better to mail it. Then he could decide, without pressure, if he wanted to get in touch with me."

"No, I'm glad I came, even if… Mom, I honestly don't know how he's going to react, but, whatever happens, I want you to know that I love you, and I'll be there for you." Her voice caught. "Brad loves you. You have Lydia and all your friends. We're your family."

"I know." Tears clogged her mother's throat. "Thank you for trying, even if…" Her voice trailed away. "I'd better go. Call me when you've spoken to him. Let him know I can't wait to hear from him."

Hayley said goodbye and hung up. When she thought of all the lost years that her mom and her uncle had missed out on, she wanted to cry. And then she thought of her own brother and a few tears did seep through her lashes. The rift that had formed between her mom and Gordon could happen to her and Brad. Over the past year, he'd been away more and more. She called him less and less. The last time they'd spoken, she'd been angry with him, and he'd seemed distracted and unconcerned. What if something happened to him over there in the Philippines? What if she never got a chance to make things right or to see him again?

She turned on the TV and switched channels until she found CNN. The cyclone had stalled over the outer islands and was continuing to wreak havoc, leaving hundreds dead and thousands homeless. Images of military aircraft unloading medical and food aid highlighted Brad's efforts in coordinating food and shelter for the victims of the disaster. He might not be great at communicating with his family, but his heart was in the right place.

As a big brother, he used to counsel her when she had problems. She missed that. If he was here now, she would ask him if she should come clean with Blake and tell him everything. Part of her really wanted to do that, but she wasn't thinking clearly and wasn't sure it was the best course of action or what all the ramifications might be. Brad was a guy; he might know better how another guy might respond to such a confession.

Without stopping to think about the time difference, she punched in the international codes and hit his number on speed dial. It rang and rang. Just when she was about to give up, he answered.

"What's up?" Brad said, his words clipped.

"Oh, Brad, it's so good to hear your voice," she said. "I've got myself in a bit of a pickle. You see, I've tracked down Mom's long-lost brother, Gordon, in Montana, but I haven't told him who I am yet. And there's this other guy, Blake, who works for him, but he seems suspicious of me. I want to tell him the truth but I just don't know—"

"Whoa, Hayley, this sounds intense," Brad broke in. "But I was asleep, finally. And I have to get up in a few hours to find drivers to take supplies out to where they're needed. I'll call you back tomorrow afternoon when I might get a few hours off."

"But I'm seeing Blake this morning—" She listened. "Brad? Brad, are you there?"

He'd hung up.

Great. She threw her phone on the bed and dragged her hands through her hair, wanting to shriek. Instead, she put her hands back in her lap and told herself not to get upset. He's doing important work. Imagine if he called her in the middle of the night and woke her up when she had an important meeting with a client the next day. She would put him off, too, although maybe a little more tactfully. But he said he would call back. She had to be patient.

Hayley checked her watch. Blake would be here soon to take her to see the post and beam house. She wouldn't say anything to him yet about Gordon being her uncle. He was Gordon's right-hand man, and they had a much longer and closer relationship than she had with either of them. She couldn't risk Blake talking to Gordon before she had a chance to. Anyway, this trip was rapidly morphing into a real business trip for her. Finally—and if this was pathetic she didn't care—she wanted to enjoy this time with Blake.

Hayley was waiting outside the hotel when Blake pulled into the driveway. She climbed into the cab, and he handed her a coffee and a paper-wrapped cookie.

"Cream, no sugar," he said. "I'm observant too."

"Thanks." She smiled, not because she needed another coffee, or even because he'd remembered what she liked, but because they had a private joke. It seemed to bring them closer, make their business connection feel more personal. Maybe, when all this was over, they could find a way to move forward.

Blake made a left onto Finley Road and headed out of town to Finley Point, the lake on their right. Heavy clouds the color of lead hung over the water, making the surrounding snow look even whiter. The road along the shore narrowed, and Blake slowed to maneuver his truck around a sharp bend.

Glancing at his rugged profile, Hayley thought about what her mom had said about making the first move. Easier said than done. She didn't go in for casual relationships, and she suspected he didn't either. He'd said he wasn't interested in Brianna, but maybe there was another woman. She knew so little about his personal life.

"You're awfully quiet this morning," she said.

He threw her a sideways look. "Just thinking."

He didn't elaborate, and she tried to come up with ways to draw him out. "You said you grew up around here. Do you have brothers or sisters?"

"No, I'm an only child."

"Oh, right," Hayley said. "Your mother was widowed young. That must have been hard for you both."

"It was tough when I was little, but we're both good now," Blake said. "She remarried about ten years ago and now lives in Arizona. I see her once or twice a year, talk to her regularly."

"You never thought of moving there too?" Hayley asked.

"Montana is my home." Blake shrugged. "Gordon's kids and the Starr brothers are my surrogate siblings. I go to their family lunches, skiing, game nights. We hang out a lot."

"That sounds nice." She couldn't help a wistful sigh. It had been a long time since she and Brad spent time together on a regular basis.

"You close to your brother?" Blake asked.

"He's away a lot." In a few succinct sentences, she told

him about Brad's job with Doctors Without Borders. Most people assumed anyone who worked for the organization was a medic of some sort, so she always explained the importance of the logistics of any relief operation.

"You must be proud of him," Blake commented.

"I am." She was also worried and resentful, feelings she didn't want to admit to but which brought the conversation to an abrupt halt.

Silence hung in the confined space of the truck cab.

"I bet your boyfriend misses you when you go away," he said casually.

A faint smile curled the corners of her mouth. Classic fishing line.

"I'm not seeing anyone special at the moment," she said. "My mom is always on my case about that, because she wants grandchildren. But I'm in no hurry." After a pause, she asked, "Are you in a relationship?"

"I was engaged, but it didn't work out."

She digested that news in silence. How long ago? Was he still hurting over the breakup? Still pining for his ex? That might account for his reserve.

"I'm too busy with my business to date much," she added, to keep the conversation going. "When the right guy comes along, maybe I'll reconsider."

"Sounds a bit lonely," Blake said.

"I can survive just fine without a partner," she said, a touch too defensively. Maybe she wasn't as fine as she thought.

"I can tell you're independent," he said. "I'm sure you're single by choice."

"I am." Her relationships in the past hadn't progressed to marriage, either because the timing hadn't been right, or the guy hadn't been a forever kind of guy. But, deep down, she did want a richer emotional life with a man she truly loved, a man who would help her raise a family, and share all the important rituals, like hanging ornaments on the Christmas tree and opening presents on Christmas morning. She felt her throat clog. Goodness, now she was getting maudlin. Rather than give in to self-pity, she mocked herself. "It's hard having high standards."

He matched her joking tone. "Knights in shining armor not thick on the ground?"

"Not so much. Although shiny armor isn't essential."

"What is?" he asked.

"Oh, the usual laundry list of must-have personality traits," she said airily. Smart, hardworking, loyal, honest, sense of humor—all the characteristics she'd noted in Blake even in this short time. "I'll know him when I meet him."

Had she met him already? Was he sitting right beside her? But how could that be? She lived in California and had a business there. He was welded to Montana. Plus, how could she expect honesty when she wasn't being honest herself? *This wasn't who she was.* Frowning, she turned to look out the window. How had she gotten herself into this predicament?

Fluffy flakes of snow began to fall. Blake switched on his wipers. Although it was morning, the ambient light dimmed, and he turned on his headlights. The swirling white outside turned the interior of the truck's cab into a cocoon of intimacy. Exchanging personal information she normally only shared with her closest girlfriends, it was easy to forget Blake was a man she barely knew, a mere business associate. He felt like a friend. Was that the small-town influence, or did they have a real connection?

"My mom said she knew my father was the right one by the way she felt when he kissed her," Hayley said.

"What she was feeling? That's not necessarily love," Blake pointed out dryly.

"She didn't mean that. She was talking about how she felt afterward, as if the world was a rosier place." Hayley smiled dreamily. "As if all her Christmases had come at once."

Blake smiled. "I've never heard love described like that before."

Hayley let a beat go by. "What happened with your fiancée?" she asked softly.

His smile faded. "Told you. It didn't work out."

Darn, she hadn't meant to bring him down. Trying to regain the teasing tone of a moment ago, she tsked. "Men! If I was talking to a girlfriend, she would tell me all the gory details."

Blake gave a dismissive shrug. "Carrie wanted different things than I did. Luckily, we realized that before we tied the knot."

What things? Hayley wanted to ask, but he obviously didn't want to talk about it. And now he was turning off the road onto a gravel driveway that wound through fir trees to a clearing surrounding a magnificent two-story log home.

"Here we are," Blake said.

Hayley got out and breathed deeply, relishing the cool scent of the trees and the fresh air. Basic landscaping had leveled the ground and cleared the undergrowth, but not much more. Tantalizing glimpses of the lake showed through the surrounding forest.

Blake stood off to one side, frowning slightly as he gazed up at the house. Was he annoyed at her for prying?

"Sorry if I was too nosy just now," she said. "We Californians are used to spilling our guts to strangers, but to some it might seem like oversharing."

"It's okay. There really isn't much to tell."

Which only made her wonder all the harder what he was hiding. But she got the hint and changed the subject. "So tell me about this house."

His expression cleared as if flicking a switch. "Three-car garage," he said, pointing at the left side of the house. "Even if your client doesn't have three cars, the extra space comes in handy for a snowmobile and winter sports equipment."

"Never would have thought of that, but now that you

mention it, good idea," Hayley said. "I can't wait to see inside."

"You do remember it's not for sale?" Blake said.

"I won't get my hopes up," Hayley assured him, but she loved it already.

Huge round logs of yellow cedar formed the walls and posts above a wide stone porch. Coming closer, Hayley saw that the carving on the eaves looked almost Scandinavian.

"I have Norwegian ancestry on my mother's side," he said, noticing her examining them. "Norwegians love their cabins in the woods."

"It's beautiful." Why would he put his own ancestry into a home for someone else? Oh. Things fell into place. "Is this *your* house?"

He nodded. Then went ahead up the steps to the porch, clearly not prepared to elaborate.

Her mind full of questions, she followed slowly, taking note of every detail, and there were many. The logs supporting the porch roof retained part of their root systems, making them appear as if they were growing organically out of the stone base. Hayley ran a hand over the polished wood, feeling the solidity and strength. "Marvelous."

The front door was a thick slab, hand carved with birds and fish and elk with spreading antlers. "It's myrtle wood," Blake told her. "A local woodcarver made it. I saw it one day at his workshop and bought it on the spot."

"It's as if it was made for this house," Hayley said, running her fingers lightly over the intricate shapes.

"I was in the early stages of the drawings so, to some extent, I did design the house around this key feature." Blake unlocked the door and swung it open, gesturing for her to enter before him.

She stepped into a wide foyer from which doorways branched off on either side but her gaze was drawn to the great room with a cathedral ceiling and wall-to-wall windows, offering a panoramic view of the lake and, in the distance, the snow-capped Mission Range.

"Wow," she breathed. Mesmerized by the spectacular setting, she walked slowly forward. Built on a rocky point, the house almost felt as if it was floating on air, surrounded by water. An expanse of level ground between the house and the edge of the cliff could one day be seeded as a lawn and perhaps planted with flowering shrubs.

"What direction are we facing here?"

"South, more or less. It gets afternoon sun," Blake said. "There's a trail down to the beach with a dock and a small boat house."

She wanted to live here.

The sense of longing was so surprising and so intense, her body almost ached with it. This view, this room, this man, Montana… It all felt so right.

Furniture was sparse, but what was there, was high quality—a huge leather couch in deep maroon, antique mahogany dining table and matching buffet. But there were no vases or decorations or pictures on the walls.

She'd never bought her own house, because she'd never been able to decide where she wanted to live permanently. Washington, Oregon, California…all up and down the West Coast, she'd worked and rented, moving on when restlessness told her she still hadn't found her spot. Now she'd started a business based in San Diego to be near her mom, and that was fine. More than fine; it was great. But it still wasn't her heart's home.

The night of the sleigh ride, she'd said she could live in Montana, but she'd thought that had been the moonlight and the stars talking. Now that she'd seen this place, she knew it was real. She could live here. Was she going crazy? Had she fallen under some spell? She wasn't here to buy a house for herself. Or anyone else for that matter.

"Why aren't you living here?" she asked. "It's at lock-up. You've moved in some furniture. It wouldn't take a lot more to make it habitable."

Blake walked over to the picture windows. He stood, legs spread, hands clasped behind his back, gazing out at the view. "I'm picking up furniture as I find it but I want the house to be completely finished before I move in. I spend so much time working on construction sites, I don't want to live in one."

She could understand that. "Did you build it for you and your fiancée to live in?"

"What? Oh, no. She never wanted to live in a log home

in the forest. Too much wood, she said. I built it after we broke up." His smile flashed. "It was a project that became an obsession."

"You did an awesome job." Hayley gazed at the stone fireplace and the blend of textures and colors of the different woods around the room. It gave the impression of rustic at first glance, but it was actually very sophisticated. The place was unique, the nicest log home she'd seen so far, either in person or on the internet. It showed what was possible with imagination and talent. "How can there ever be too much wood? It's beautiful."

"Carrie said she felt suffocated surrounded by forest," he explained. "Now she lives on the fifteenth floor of an apartment building."

"Her loss," Hayley said, shaking her head in wonder. "Being in nature makes it all the more special."

"I think so too."

So now she knew at least one of the things he wanted from a relationship—someone who would be happy to live in this beautiful, peaceful dwelling in the woods.

"Do you want to see the rest of the house?" Blake asked. "It's a good example of how post and beam differs from the other log home construction methods."

"Of course."

He led her through the dining room to a large kitchen with sleek light brown cabinets, a walk-in pantry, and an island. A central skylight provided natural light that illuminated the pale marble counters.

"I like your color choices," Hayley said. "The logs absorb a lot of light."

"Fifty percent," Blake told her.

"That much?" Hayley said, surprised. She glanced at the hanging lights. "A rail lighting system would work well in here. My supplier has them in a warm bronze finish that would complement the logs beautifully." Seeing his raised eyebrow, she flushed lightly. "Sorry, I get carried away. I'm sure you have your own ideas."

"No, that's okay," he said. "I wasn't totally happy with the lighting. I'll think about what you said."

Blake led her on a tour of the rest of the downstairs, which comprised a home office, laundry and mud room, a TV room, and a guest bedroom. Upstairs, there were three bedrooms and the master retreat, all with lake views. Other than the four-poster bed in the master, the couch in the living room and the dining room set, the house was unfurnished.

"As you can see, although the frame is log, the walls up here are drywall which allows more leeway when it comes to decorating," Blake said.

"It's nice to have the flexibility," Hayley agreed. "Brianna mentioned western furniture for log homes, but I like how you've gotten inventive with the four-poster and the antique dining room furniture," she said. "One thing is for sure, you need large pieces to match the proportions of the house.

Decorating this place would be fun. It has a really good feel."

"There's a basement that I intend to turn into a rec room, but it's not finished yet."

"I'd love to see it," she said.

They went back downstairs to a door in the hall between the kitchen and the mud room. The stairway was steep and the light dim. Hayley gripped the rail and followed Blake down. At the bottom, he turned to give her a hand. "The floor isn't in so watch out for the last step."

She could have managed by herself, but she put her hand in his. His clasp was firm, his fingers warm. She landed safely and found herself standing close to him. Still he held her hand and waited while her eyes adjusted to the low light.

"Okay?" he said. When she nodded, he released her.

Hayley immediately wanted to reach for his hand again. She wasn't afraid of dark spaces with low ceilings, but she didn't exactly love them either. She stuck close as they moved past the hot water heater and into an open area. He flipped a switch, and a bare light bulb hanging from the ceiling glowed yellow, casting shadows.

"I'm thinking about putting a pool table in here," he said.

"Or ping-pong," she suggested.

"Sure, why not," he said. "Both."

"And shuffleboard."

"Not sure there's enough room," he said. "How about a dart board?"

"Sounds good." She turned to smile at him, and he smiled back. For a moment, it felt as if they were planning the future in that house together. There would be kids and dogs and a lot of noise and family fun.

It was such a beguiling mental image that she almost couldn't bear it. Needing a distraction, she looked at her watch. "I've taken up a lot of your time. It's nearly noon."

"Not a problem." But the moment of closeness had passed. They went back upstairs. Blake locked up, did a quick check that all lights were off, and they went outside to the truck.

"Thank you for showing me your home," Hayley said.

She gave the house one last lingering glance as they left. It really was the most incredibly beautiful home she'd ever seen. Even though she'd only spent a half hour here, she wished she could have a lifetime. Someday, Blake would find a wife, and live here with his family and have all those things she longed for. Why did that make her so sad?

Chapter Eight

Wednesday, December 18, continued

B LAKE PEERED THROUGH the windshield wipers at the road ahead. Snow was falling more heavily now and starting to stick to the road, an inch or more deep in spots. The plows would be out tonight.

Beside him, Hayley seemed lost in thought. That she'd liked his house made him feel surprisingly good. He knew it was a fine building, both architecturally and aesthetically, but it meant something to have her say so. As an interior designer, he respected her professional opinion. More than that, he liked her, so it mattered to him that she admired his house. He'd poured everything he had into it—time, emotions, savings, and energy—for two years.

"Did you ever get chains?" he asked Hayley as they approached town.

"No." Worriedly, she peered through the side window at the accumulating white stuff. "I shouldn't have procrastinated, but it's been so sunny that I hoped the forecast would be wrong."

"Here's the thing about winter in Montana," he said, only half joking. "If there are clouds in the sky in December, it's either snowing, or it's going to snow soon."

"Here's the thing about living in Southern California," she admitted. "I don't know how to put chains on. Or when to put them on. Or how to take them off. In short, they are a complete mystery to me."

"No reason you should know all that. I can show you." He took a right on Main and another on Fourth Avenue to Brand's Auto. "Wait here."

He headed over to the mechanic's bay where Damon Brand, in navy coveralls, was working under a car up on the hoist. "Hey, bud. Have you got a set of chains to fit a 2016 Mercedes GLC?"

Damon put the wrench down and wiped his hands on a rag. "I should. Let's go have a look inside."

Hayley caught up with them as Blake followed Damon into the garage. "Does he have some?"

"He's checking," Blake said.

Damon scanned the shelves at the back and returned with a package of chains. "These will do the trick."

Hayley came inside as Damon was ringing up the sale, and Blake introduced them.

"No snow tires?" Damon asked her.

"I'm from California," she said, handing over her credit card.

"That explains it," Damon said. "You need help putting

them on?"

"I've got it," Blake said. "Catch you later."

Blake drove Hayley back to the hotel. An employee was shoveling the path in front of the building, but hadn't yet gotten to the parking lot.

"Are you going anywhere today?" Blake asked.

"Nowhere I can't walk to," she said. "Tomorrow I'm picking up Brianna to go shopping. Do you think the roads will be plowed by then?"

"Possibly, but if it keeps snowing, they might not be clear when you want to go," Blake said. "We'll put the chains on, and if you don't need them in the morning, you can take them off again."

He showed her how to line up her tires, drape the chains over the wheel and drive a couple of feet before fastening them snugly. He then showed her how to remove them. Finally, he got her to practice by herself until she was able to do it without instruction.

"All right, I'd better get back to work." He dusted off his gloved hands. "You'll be fine, don't worry. Anything goes wrong, you've got my number."

"Thanks, Blake," she said. "I appreciate this."

"It's nothing," he said. "You can teach me how to surf next time I'm in San Diego."

"You got it," she said, then grinned. "As soon as I learn how."

Her smile was infectious, and Blake found himself grinning back. They'd shared some confidences this morning, and he felt as if he was getting to know her. His rule about not dating clients, even potential ones, suddenly seemed pointlessly restrictive. "Do you feel like getting lunch?"

At first, her face lit up, and then she seemed to think twice. "I don't like to mix business with pleasure."

So she considered lunch with him a pleasure and not just business. That was encouraging. "We can talk about how you plan to stage the spec home, if that makes it more business and less pleasure. Or, you could tell me exactly what your client is looking for. That way, I could show you some sample floor plans next time we meet."

A flush came into Hayley's cheeks. "Uh, sure."

Why did she look so guilty every time he mentioned her client? The obvious answer leaped out at him. She didn't have one, at least not one that was looking for a log home near Sweetheart, Montana.

"What is it, Hayley?" he asked quietly. "What aren't you telling me?" He liked her, and didn't want to upset her. But he had to know.

Her eyes searched his face, and she bit her lip, as though to stop herself from bursting out with whatever it was she was hiding. For a moment, he thought she would actually say it.

Tell me, he willed her. *Don't make this hard.*

Still, she said nothing.

"Are you working for John Coates?" The words came out

of his mouth before he could stop himself.

"I beg your pardon?" she said, frowning.

"Coates Construction," he said. "Are you working for him?"

"No. I work for myself," she said. "I don't understand why you keep bringing him up. Or why you think I would be working for him. I'm from California. You've seen my website."

"You might be working for him on the side," Blake said. "He's opening an office in Sacramento. It's a long way from San Diego but still."

"What are you getting at?" she asked.

Too late, he wished he'd never started this conversation. "He employs people to investigate companies he's interested in investing in."

"You mean like a spy?" she said, eyes wide. "You think I'm a spy?"

"You've been asking a lot of questions about Gordon, about the company, how the business is doing. I just thought—"

"No," she said, shaking her head. "I'm not spying for this John Coates. I wouldn't do that. I—" She broke off, looking stricken.

"What?" he asked.

"Nothing." She bit her lip, clearly still upset. "If you'll excuse me, I have a lot of work to do this afternoon. Thanks again for showing me the house, and for helping me with the chains. You've really gone above and beyond."

"No problem." Snow was falling faster now, swirling in the gusts of cold air off the lake. He hunched his shoulders against the wind.

"I…I'll see you later." She touched his arm briefly before turning to hurry up the paved walk to the hotel.

Blake watched her go. He didn't know what to think anymore. She'd denied spying for Coates, and he believed her. She was helping them by doing the staging. And, yet, there was still something not quite right, some piece missing from the puzzle that was Hayley Stevens.

He got in his truck, but instead of heading back to the office, he decided to get a quick burger at the tavern. When he pushed open the door, the warmth hit him with a welcome blast. The muted TV over the bar was tuned to a hockey game, and the click of pool balls in the corner mingled with music on the jukebox.

It was some cowboy song about being fooled by the woman he loved. Carrie had fooled him into thinking she wanted what he wanted—marriage, a home in Sweetheart, children. At the end, it had become all too apparent that she didn't want any of those things, and never had.

He signaled to the bartender for a draft beer. He didn't know what game Hayley was playing, but he'd been duped by a woman once. He didn't plan on getting fooled again.

Hayley walked swiftly through the lobby and up the staircase to the second floor. She felt terrible. All morning she and Blake had been getting along like old friends, exchanging confidences, joking together. He'd gotten her the chains and showed her how to put them on—a huge help. He'd invited her to lunch, and she'd wanted so badly to sit across a table in some cozy cafe and continue to get to know him.

And then he'd accused her of being a spy for a rival business.

He was wrong, but it showed he knew she was hiding something. Telling him the truth would have been such a sweet relief, but, as well as they were getting along, she still couldn't be sure if he would be an ally who would help her obtain a private meeting with Gordon, or if he would treat her as a foe, defending his boss against the cast-aside sister. She wished she knew why her uncle had turned his back on her mom, what grudge he'd held all these years. But she couldn't tell anyone else her true purpose here until she told Gordon. It was private, not for anyone else's ears.

At the top of the landing, she slowed her pace as she walked along the gallery to her room. What to do now? The sensible thing would be to order room service and spend the afternoon planning out what she would need for staging the spec home.

But Blake had planted a seed in her brain with his talk of spying and she couldn't let go of the thought that John

Coates posed some kind of threat to her uncle's company. She'd been so shocked at the spying allegation that she hadn't had the presence of mind to ask what was going on, although Blake probably wouldn't have told her anyway. Maybe she should go see Coates. She might be able to bring back some information that could help Gordon's company—and redeem herself in Blake's eyes.

Coates was in Polson, and it was snowing. Had the highway been plowed yet? Well, so what if it hadn't? Have chains, will travel.

She hurried back downstairs and went out to her car, looking on her phone for the address of Coates Construction. A check of the map showed the town was less than twenty minutes southwest of Sweetheart. According to Wikipedia, it was double the size of Sweetheart, which was still small, and would be easy to get around.

She headed out along Finley Road toward the junction with the highway. The chains made a disconcertingly loud clatter whenever she hit a clear patch of road where wind had blown the powdery snow away, but mostly the road noise was muffled by a couple of inches of snow. The plow was coming down Finley Road from the other direction, which gave her hope that Route 35 would be clear.

The highway had been plowed earlier, but another layer of fresh snow was accumulating rapidly. Wipers flapping on high speed, she drove carefully at a reasonable speed and made it without incident to Polson. With a sense of relief, she pulled into the small parking lot outside the offices of Coates Construction. Taking a moment to let the blood return to her white knuckles, she reveled in a quiet sense of triumph over the elements. As a SoCal gal, being able to drive in snow felt like a small superpower.

She pushed open the glass door and entered a deathly quiet reception area. The young brunette seated behind the counter wore a thin pink cardigan that clung to her buxom figure. Surely her clothing was too skimpy for the cold climate. Plugged in to an earphone, she tapped briskly at the computer keys, not hearing the bell over the door.

Hayley glanced around. Standard issue office décor. The colors in the bland artwork matched the carpet and upholstery on the guest seating. If the office at Sweetheart Log Homes was like a quirky local cafe, this was like walking into a generic corporate headquarters. It made her wonder if the homes built by Coates Construction had as little personality.

"Excuse me," she said to the receptionist who, according to her nameplate, was called Dani. "I'm interested in having a log home built. Is Mr. Coates in?"

Dani paused her audio stream, trying, but not succeeding, in hiding her impatience. "He's busy."

"Do you have a model house or any spec homes I could view?" Hayley persisted.

Dani pushed a real estate flyer at her from the pile on the counter. "A couple of our homes are for sale. You need to make an appointment through the local Realtor to view them."

Hayley picked up the flyer with a cursory glance. "If I wanted a new home built would you design it to my specifications?"

"You can choose from one of six standard models." Dani's hands remained poised over the keyboard, ready to continue as soon as Hayley stopped interrupting her. "A limited number of modifications are available, but they cost extra."

"Can you tell me the average price of one of your homes new?" Hayley persisted. "And how long is the wait time?"

"You'll have to speak to one of our salesmen about that." Dani gave a just audible sigh, picked up a pen and turned to an appointment book. "Name and contact number? Someone will give you a call."

"That's okay," Hayley said. "I'll look at these and get back to you if I decide to go further." There was no point giving her details when she wasn't really interested. "Thanks for your help." Not.

As she turned to leave, the door behind the reception desk opened and out came a man about fifty years old, good-looking in a flashy way. He wore a cashmere coat over an expensive suit and a large gold watch. "How's that letter coming, Dani?"

"Almost done, Mr. Coates." Dani smiled prettily.

Hayley resumed her slow progress toward the exit, glancing over her shoulder. So this was the owner of the company,

John Coates. He touched the receptionist's shoulder lightly, his gaze drifting down to the open top buttons of her cardigan.

"I'll be back around two," he went on. "Did you get a meeting time arranged with Gordon Renton?"

Hearing her uncle's name, Hayley lingered by the door, taking her time to find her car keys in her purse. Why exactly was Blake worried about Coates spying on them? What did Coates want with Gordon? Business, or were they friends?

"Yes, sir," Dani said. "Nine thirty, Friday morning. At his office, just like you said."

"Excellent," he said briskly. "I'll be back in an hour."

As Coates approached the door where she was loitering, Hayley caught a whiff of his overpowering cologne and took a step back to make way for him.

"Are you on your way out?" he guessed, gesturing to the flyer and the keys in her hand. When she nodded, he held the door open.

"Thanks." She went out and breathed deeply of the welcome fresh air.

"I'm John Coates," he said as they moved down the short path toward the parking lot. "Are you interested in buying a log home?"

"Hayley," she said. "Yes, I am."

"Good to meet you, Hayley. You've come to the right place." His slick smile firmly in place, his gaze flicked over her, assessing her clothes and hair. "You look too upmarket

to be a local. Slightly tanned in December. Let me guess—
L.A., Santa Barbara?" He gave her a wink. "Am I getting
warm?"

"Right state, wrong cities." Disliking the man instinctive-
ly, she had no wish now to prolong the conversation. Blake
had implied she knew this man well. It was almost insulting.
"It was nice to meet you."

"I'm over here too. That must be your Mercedes with the
California plates," he said. "San Diego, Hayley?"

She forced a smile. "Bingo."

"Wonderful city. So, Hayley, did you get everything you
needed from Dani?"

She wished he would stop saying her name. "Not really. I
was hoping to view some homes, but your receptionist told
me to see the local Realtors."

His mouth twitched in annoyance, then returned to a
smile. "Dani's a great girl. I apologize if she wasn't overly
helpful. I gave her an urgent task this morning."

"That's okay," Hayley said. "I'm in no hurry to buy."

"We have a magnificent two story up in Kalispell, and a
ranch style near Missoula," John said. "Give me your
number, and I'll get my top salesman to call you right away."

"No, thank you. Those are farther away than I wanted,"
she said. "I'm looking more locally, up toward the town of
Sweetheart."

"Well, as a matter of fact..." His chest beneath the fine-
textured coat expanded ever so slightly. "I'm beginning

negotiations to buy out another log home company. Soon we may have more inventory."

"Oh?" Hayley said politely as a virtual alarm bell started ringing.

"Right there in Sweetheart, as a matter of fact," he went on. "They've been around a while and have quite a few homes for sale."

Hayley hid her shock. Neither Gordon nor Blake had so much as hinted that they might be on the verge of selling the company. But why, when the business seemed to be thriving?

"Sweetheart Log Homes?" she asked, just to be sure.

"Yes, but don't bother going to see them. They likely won't be in business long. A bit rinky dink, if you know what I mean. Family run, small town, small time," John waved a hand disparagingly. "Coates Construction is the largest commercial and retail construction company in the state of Montana. We have offices in Idaho and Oregon, and I'm expanding to California. Better you should wait and buy from us. Bigger company, better service."

She could argue that point, but didn't want to engage with him any longer than necessary. "When is this takeover happening?"

"Soon, very soon," he said. "We haven't come to an agreement yet, but I don't anticipate any difficulties. The owner is getting on, and his children aren't interested in carrying on the business. His manager isn't in a position to take over."

"How do you know that?" Blake and Gordon would be appalled if he heard Coates talking this way about them.

"I have my sources." John tapped the side of his nose.

"I see." Holding up her keys, she took a step away. "Well, I need to get going."

Coates pulled out a business card and scribbled a number on the back. "That's my personal cell number. When you've seen the rest, come and see the best." He chuckled at his own wit. "I'd be happy to personally show you around."

"Very nice of you." She took the card. *Thanks, but no thanks.* "Bye now."

Quickly, before he could start talking again, she got in her car and drove off. Shaken from the encounter, she didn't pause to think about which direction she was taking. If her first reaction to the news that Gordon was selling his business had been shock, the second was indignation. How could he, in good conscience, do business with her, when he might not own the company soon? And Blake obviously knew what was going on. He should have warned her.

Her hands gripped the steering wheel hard as she sped up a bit to get through the intersection on an orange light. Once a contract was entered into, construction of a new home took months. When was her uncle planning to mention the sale of his business, before or after her client signed the contract to buy a home from them? Yes, okay, the client wasn't real, but they didn't know that.

No wonder, though, that Gordon was stressed. The dark

circles and lines of fatigue made sense now. He'd worked all his life to build a legacy, and now it was about to pass out of his hands. Was it something he wanted, or not?

With all these thoughts clouding her brain, it was a good ten minutes before she noticed that the lake was on her right when it should be on her left if she was heading back to Sweetheart. Moreover, the road she was driving on hadn't been plowed. She'd taken a wrong turn in town and was now heading north on the opposite side of the lake. Worse, there was nowhere to turn around. She crept along the narrow, winding road. The snow was coming down thicker and faster than ever.

Thank goodness Blake had helped her to put chains on. Although if she hadn't had chains, she would never have ventured out in the first place. But, then, she never would have found out about John Coates taking over her uncle's business.

Between the ever-deepening snow, her worry over Gordon and his business, and her disgust for John Coates, the tension in her hands gripping the wheel seeped into her whole body. Before long, her leg ached with alternating between accelerator and brake, and her head pounded with the effort of concentrating on staying on the road and not drifting over the narrow shoulder. Now and then she would round a bend and find herself mere feet from a drop-off of the rocky shoreline. How long was the drive in this direction? In good weather on a clear road, probably not more than a couple of hours.

Every side road or driveway she passed, she slowed, debating whether to try to turn around. But the snow was coming so thickly, and the visibility was so bad, that her heart started palpitating at the thought of a truck coming upon her suddenly in the middle of turning around. On she went, following the road north around the lake, trusting that sooner or later, she would come full circle and end up back in Sweetheart. Unless she took another wrong turn, easy to do in this blizzard.

To take her mind off the danger and uncertainty, she mulled over her encounter with John Coates. He was a man full to overflowing with his own self-importance. Maybe he was mistaken, and her uncle had no intention of selling. Even if Gordon was going to sell, he was under no obligation to tell her anything about his business dealings. Who was she to him? As far as he knew, she was only browsing the log home market. If and when she brought him a firm offer from her client, no doubt he would reveal his plans.

Shame washed over her. There was no client. She'd been here only a few days, but it felt as if she'd been carrying this falsehood around with her for a lifetime. What had seemed at first like a small, unimportant deception, had mushroomed out of control. She hated not being truthful, all the more so to people she liked and who were being so nice to her. It was one thing to not reveal the full truth to someone like John Coates, whom she didn't know and wasn't ever going to see again. But Gordon was her uncle and a sweetheart, and Brianna a doll.

And Blake... He'd opened up to her about his ex-fiancée and showed her his dream house. Her heart hurt for him when she thought of his ex running off to the city and leaving him. When he knew how Hayley had kept the real purpose of her trip hidden, he would have every right to be angry with her.

A settlement of houses along the lakeshore came into view through the falling snow. The town sign read, Somers. She was at the northernmost end of the lake. She tanked up on gas, got a burger from a drive-through fast-food restaurant, and braced herself for the last long leg of her journey. The road wasn't any better on this side of the lake. If anything, it was worse. So much for her small superpower. Rookie mistake, setting out on a long, unnecessary, road trip in a snowstorm, even with chains.

When finally, hours later, she drove into the parking lot at the Montreau Hotel in Sweetheart, she almost wept with relief. Gone was any sense of triumph, only a feeling of being humbled by nature. She was exhausted physically and mentally.

She trudged up the stairs to her room and had a long, hot shower. Donning her pajamas, she ordered pasta from room service. As she ate, she remembered that Brad was going to call her this afternoon. She checked her phone. No call. Typical. Well, that was it. She wasn't going to call him again.

Turning in early, she found a radio station playing quiet carols, and put out the light. Tired as she was, she couldn't get to sleep for thinking about how, if her mom and her uncle did manage to reconcile, she would likely be visiting here on a regular basis. Before she left Sweetheart, she would have apologized to Blake for wasting his time. And to Brianna for not telling her who she was. She moaned aloud, now fully awake again.

She glanced at the bedside clock and sat up. It was only eight p.m. Way too early to go to sleep. And she had too much on her mind to sit quietly in her room and stare at the TV.

She got up and dressed. A nightcap might be just the thing.

Chapter Nine

Wednesday evening, December 18

B LAKE SPENT THE afternoon finishing his design for a tiny home. It was to be post and beam with a shake roof and a drywall interior. He was really excited by the challenge of working maximum storage into a minimum space. But it had been difficult to focus with the scene with Hayley playing over and over in his mind. After an upbeat morning getting to know her better, renewing his pleasure in his house on Finley Point, and working together on the snow chains, she'd been at the point of accepting his lunch invitation when he'd gone and accused her of spying for the opposition. Not only had he risked losing a client, he'd damaged their blossoming friendship.

Darkness had fallen, and the snow had stopped by the time he headed home to the two-bedroom rental on Sweet Street. It was comfortable enough, but only a stopgap until he could move into his log home. Going through the house today with Hayley had reminded him how much he loved that place and how much of himself he'd put into every nook and cranny. Not long now before he could move in. A month, maybe two. He was counting the days.

He went to the kitchen, Rebel padding at his heels. He fed the dog, then rummaged in the fridge for something to eat. Cold pizza? Pass.

Restless, he went out back to load up a basket of wood for the woodburning stove in the living room, which provided most of the heat and all of the atmosphere. He chucked a few logs on the banked coals and blew on the embers, then sat back on his haunches and studied the flames.

His thoughts drifted to taking Hayley's hand in the basement. Her skin felt so soft in his. And the way she'd smiled during their little exchange about the games room, as if they were planning it together. It had been so easy to imagine they'd connected on a personal level. He was attracted to Hayley, and he was pretty sure she felt the chemistry too. Then, just when they were getting along so well, he'd gone and screwed up. Was Brianna right, was he scared of getting involved with a woman again?

"I didn't even stop to wonder why Hayley would go to the trouble of doing the staging if she was a spy," he said to Rebel. "What's wrong with me?"

Rebel's eyebrows twitched, and he repositioned his muzzle on his paws, but made no comment.

"Thing is, boy, I learned the hard way not to trust women," Blake went on. "With Carrie, I was blinded by my feelings and didn't recognize that she was planning to pull a dirty on me. So now I look for trouble where there is none."

Blake fed another log onto the flames, closed up the stove, got a beer, and retreated to the couch. Rebel lay on his mat in front of the heat from the stove, half an eye open to keep watch over his master.

"On the other hand, I still think there's something off-kilter about Hayley. Maybe I'm wrong about her working for Coates, but something doesn't add up, something she's not telling. It's going to be great having her stage the house and, god knows, I like having her around. But I still think it's odd that she agreed to do it. Right?"

Again, Rebel offered no opinion on the matter, so Blake outlined his reasoning. "As a busy professional—and judging by her website, she has plenty of business back home—she shouldn't have time to potter around, staging a log home that she might not even recommend to her client to buy. And, if she *was* going to recommend it, why bother going to the trouble of decorating it so someone else might buy it first? But what am I going to do, tell her no? Not hardly. If it's a ruse, it's a pretty elaborate one."

Rebel made a low noise in his throat, not quite a rumble, not quite a growl, but it sounded a little like he was agreeing.

"I just hope like heck that whatever I do find out about her won't be bad news," Blake went on. "Because, at the same time as I suspect she's hiding something, I'm falling for her. Yeah, I know, crazy, right?"

But, after what had happened today, no doubt Hayley

couldn't stand him. Would it be wrong now to ask her for the name of her supplier of the rail lighting she'd mentioned for his kitchen? It might be a good excuse to call her.

"I know what you're thinking, Reb. I should apologize, not ask for more favors." Blake checked his watch. Seven thirty p.m. He reached for his phone and then thought better of calling. The personal touch was always the best. "I could swing by the hotel, like it's a spur of the moment thing, see if she wants to have a drink, maybe follow that with dinner. What do you think, Rebel?"

The dog's eyes were closed, and his mouth slightly parted in sleep. Blake took his pet's relaxed demeanor as confirmation that he was finally on the right track. He put down his half-drunk beer and got to his feet. Rebel lifted his head, eyes half-open as he wakened from his slumber. Bending to pat him, Blake said, "You stay here, buddy. I spend too much time talking to you as it is. No offense, but there are times when you cramp my style."

He showered, shaved and changed into clean chinos and a fresh chambray shirt. He would do himself no good showing up looking like a lumberjack.

At the hotel, he called Hayley from the lobby but her phone was busy so he asked the guy at the desk to call her on the housephone so he could at least leave a message. No answer. With all the snow, she likely hadn't gone far. Blake went looking for her in the restaurant. Not there. A few more steps took him to the bar. He paused in the doorway.

She was seated on a stool, just putting down her phone. As he watched, she chatted with the bartender and sipped from a glass of white wine. In her dark red wool dress, heeled ankle boots, and blonde hair waving around her shoulders, she looked utterly delectable.

From the doorway, Blake dialed her number again.

She reached for her phone on the bar, saw his number, and hesitated long enough for the breath he was holding to tighten his chest. She hadn't seen him. Would she pick up?

At last she did. "Can I help you?"

"I'd like to buy you a drink."

"Sorry, I just washed my hair," she replied coolly. "I'm in my pajamas, getting ready for a night in with Netflix."

"Is that so? Lady, you lie as smoothly as a fitted sheet." He started walking toward her. "How about putting on that nice red dress of yours, slipping on some warm boots, and heading downstairs to the bar? I'm thinking you'd enjoy a glass of Pinot Grigio. Or maybe Chardonnay."

She froze. And then turned slowly around. Her gaze slammed into his, and her cheeks went red. Busted.

He walked over and slid onto the stool next to hers. "So, to repeat my question, will you have a drink with me?"

"Do I have a choice?"

"Of course. Say the word, and I'll leave this minute."

"Stay," she said. "Just don't act smug because you caught me lying."

"Oh, come on now. That's not fair," he said silkily. "I

think I deserve just the tiniest of edge of an upper hand when I'm about to grovel."

She raised a supercilious eyebrow. "Fine then. Grovel away."

Blake dropped the act. "I apologize for how I spoke to you this morning. I had no right, or reason, to accuse you of spying for John Coates."

"No need for an apology," Hayley said. "I understand why you're worried."

"Oh?" he said. That was an unexpected reaction.

"Coates wants to take over your company."

"How do you know?" Blake asked. "Did Brianna tell you?"

"No, John Coates himself did. I went to Polson this afternoon and spoke to him." She shuddered. "I promise you, I'm not working for that odious man."

Blake gave a small smile. "He has that effect on some women." Then he sobered. "The buyout or takeover, whatever you want to call it, is only a possibility. Gordon hasn't made a decision one way or the other yet, as far as I know. Please don't say anything to anyone."

"I won't," Hayley said.

"Your client doesn't need to worry," Blake assured her. "Nothing would happen immediately. If she were to purchase a house from Sweetheart Log Homes, we would honor that commitment."

"That's good to know," Hayley said. "My offer to stage

the spec home still stands."

"Also good to know." Relieved that the air had been cleared, he signaled to the bartender and ordered a beer. "So, the California girl drove to Polson in a snowstorm. Tell me about it."

"Oh, my god!" She put her hands up and covered her face briefly. "I was okay going there, but on the way back, I took a wrong turn and ended up going the long way around the lake. The experience has scarred me for life."

He had to laugh. "Lucky you had chains."

"I never would have gone if it wasn't for the chains!" She nudged his leg with her foot. "They made me overconfident."

"But you made it," he said. "Well done for that."

"Yes, I survived, but afterward I curled under the covers, a gibbering idiot." She sipped her wine. "For a while."

"And you met John Coates," Blake added more soberly. "I'm surprised he told a complete stranger that he's taking over our company. He's meeting with Gordon and me on Friday, but it's far from a done deal."

"He's cocky," Hayley said. "I wasn't very interested in what they had to offer. He may only have been trying to impress a potential client."

"Trying to impress an attractive woman," Blake amended.

She shrugged away the compliment but her hand moved closer to his on the bar until the tips of their fingers almost, but not quite, touched. "I take it you don't want the business sold to him."

"Not to anyone. But John Coates, especially, would be bad for the company, bad for the employees, bad for the whole town."

She hesitated. "Coates said that, if Gordon retired, you wouldn't be able to buy him out."

"He actually said that?" Outrageous. How did Coates know anything about his personal finances? The man's arrogance made Blake want to block him even more. But he didn't want to get into that right now. The bartender arrived with his beer. Blake turned to Hayley. "Another wine?"

"I'd better not. I need to get up early to meet Brianna," Hayley said. "Tonight I'm going to draw up a rough plan and list the essentials."

"You're really going out of your way for us," he said. "Don't get me wrong, we're very grateful, but why are you doing this?"

"I told you, this will take my business in a new direction. There are log homes in Northern California, Oregon, Washington. I work all over the place. Heck, I would even come to Montana again." She paused. "If you don't trust me…"

"No, it's not that," he protested. But it was, really.

"Everything will become clear with time," she said.

In other words, there *was* more to it than growing her business. But he wasn't going to get any more out of her now.

"The rooms of the spec home and my house are roughly

the same size," Blake said. "If you think my furniture would work, I could have it moved over tomorrow."

"That would be fantastic," Hayley said. "You have excellent taste. I'll keep the soft furnishings simple, since time is limited—mine as well as yours," she said. "Plus you might not have a big budget for a spec home."

"Get what you need. If we end up staging more houses, I'm sure we'll use it." Or, if her taste matched his as well as it seemed to, he might buy some items off the company for his house. "You can invoice us for your time."

"Whatever," she said, waving a hand as if dismissing the notion. "When is the open house again?"

"Saturday," he said.

"That's tight, but it can be done." She smiled. "Deal?"

Blake put out his hand. "Deal."

His fingers closed around hers, and he held on a little longer than necessary. She met his gaze and didn't look away. He could swear he wasn't the only one who felt the undercurrents of something more personal in their interactions.

"Would you like to go skiing?" he found himself asking. "After the staging, of course."

"If I'm still here, that would be wonderful."

That brought him down to earth with a bang. If she was still here. Women had a habit of leaving. He needed to remember that.

Or, he could try to convince her to stay.

Chapter Ten

Thursday morning, December 19

T HE ALARM RANG at six thirty a.m. Bare toes curling on the cold floorboards, he threw a couple of logs into the woodstove, blew the banked embers to life, and went back to bed until the house warmed up a little.

Seeing that his master was awake, if not up, Rebel left his cozy bed to sit next to Blake's. Blake hung an arm over the side of the bed to pat him, and the dog licked his wrist. Now that was true loyalty. If Carrie had felt a fraction of the loyalty toward him that his dog did…

Blake stopped his mind before it went down that old worn groove through sheer habit. The truth was, he no longer cared about losing Carrie. He'd been assuring everyone that was the case for so long and, finally, it was true. He felt as if he'd been plagued by a toothache, only to wake up and find the pain was gone. Pure relief.

He'd intended to doze another half hour, but now he was wide awake, his thoughts turning to Hayley. He still didn't know what was going on with her, but she was on

Gordon's side which, as far as Blake was concerned, opened the way for a real relationship. If they had the chance to go skiing, she would need ski equipment, so he would drop in on Garrett on his way to work. So much for his rule about not dating clients, but that had been an excuse all along, hadn't it?

Blake got dressed, had a quick breakfast, and headed out to Garrett's store, Outdoor Adventures. Fortunately, his friend was another early bird, and the lights were on. He parked around the back and, leaving Rebel in the truck, entered the store through the loading bay, edging past stacked bundles of tents and other camping gear to emerge into the bright shop. "Garrett, are you here?"

"Out front," Garrett called. He was stocking snowboard wax on a display shelf. He wore a puffer vest over a checked flannel shirt, and his thick dark hair flopped over a high forehead. "You're up early. There's a layer of awesome fresh snow out there. Are you taking the day off work to go skiing?"

"Nah, just checking to see if you have any cross-country skis available for rent this weekend," Blake said.

"Sure, what size?" Garrett said.

"To fit a woman about five foot eight," Blake said. "Nothing too fast. She's a beginner."

Garrett set down the box of wax tubs and headed for the storeroom at the back. "Let's see what I've got."

In the storeroom, Garrett picked out a pair of long, sleek

skis, black with red detailing. "I'm going up to Blacktail on Sunday with Liz from the florist. Want to tag along?"

"That sounds good," Blake said. "So are you seeing Liz now?" Garrett was a little like him, never dating the same woman for long. Not because he was gun-shy like Blake, but more because he was content to play the field.

"Nah, we're just friends." Garrett leaned on a pile of boxes containing ice skates. "What about you? Who are these for?"

"Hayley," Blake said. "She's here to scout out a log home for a client back in California."

"Is that the pretty blonde you were with at my parents' open house?" Garrett asked.

"Not 'with' exactly," Blake said. "I've been showing her log homes."

"Oh, is that what it's called these days?" his friend replied with a knowing grin.

"No harm in making her feel welcome," Blake said, feeling self-conscious.

"The least you can do," Garret agreed, tongue in cheek. "Nice, is she?"

"She's fun and smart. And she has…presence. Something about her draws you in." Blake felt heat climbing into his cheeks. "It's hard to put into words."

"You've got a thing for her," Garrett said, ribbing him. "Blushing like a schoolboy."

"Don't be ridiculous." Blake cleared his throat and attempted to sound businesslike. "She's an interior designer, helping us stage a house. I'd like to make her stay in town a pleasant one."

"Oh, I'm sure you'll do that," Garret said knowingly.

"Get your mind out of the gutter." Blake got him in a headlock and, for a moment, they engaged in a friendly tussle until they knocked over a bunch of skis propped against the wall. Blake let go and backed away.

Garrett smoothed his shirt down. "Will she need any clothing for Saturday? Ski pants, gloves…?"

"I didn't think of that, but probably." Blake picked up a pair of socks that had fallen to the floor and replaced them on the hook. "She'll want to pick her own out."

"Okay, tell her to come in any time," Garrett said.

"I'll do that. I'll hang onto these for a few days." Blake hoisted the skis under his arm. "Catch you later."

Garrett followed him out to the parking lot and stood in the doorway, grinning. "Blake's got it b-ad," he said in a singsong voice.

Blake rolled his eyes and placed the skis into the back of his truck. "Get a life, Starr." Then he sobered, all joking aside. "Bottom line, she lives in California. She'll be going back there."

Garrett's smile faded, too. "Don't get in too deep, bro. You're not, right?"

With a noncommittal shrug, Blake lifted a hand in farewell. "Catch you later."

HAYLEY MET BRIANNA at the office at eight o'clock to go to the Antiques Barn. Brianna drove, and as they headed north on Route 35, Hayley went over the lists of items she'd drawn up for the various rooms, using her photos and the floor plan that Blake had emailed to her yesterday as a guide. Finally, she closed her folder. She'd been as thorough as possible. No doubt there would be the odd thing she'd forgotten, but she had tomorrow and Saturday morning to tie up loose ends.

"It doesn't have to be perfect," Brianna said. "As long as we do the main rooms, Dad will be happy."

"When do you expect him back?" Hayley asked.

"Not 'til late tonight," Brianna said. "It's a long drive. He has to be back, though, because he's got a meeting first thing tomorrow morning."

"With John Coates?" Hayley asked.

"Did Blake tell you about that?" Brianna said curiously.

Hayley nodded. "I went to Polson to check out Coates's log homes. I didn't get to see any, but, after meeting him, I didn't want to. I wasn't very impressed with him, frankly."

Brianna made a face. "Just between you and me, he's a jerk."

The spec home came up on the right, and Brianna slowed. "Do you want to have another look?"

"I've got enough information to go on." Hayley paused. "Do you think your father will sell his business?"

"I really don't know," Brianna said, resuming normal speed. "I know Mom would like him to retire, but Dad still enjoys working. And he doesn't want his company to go to John Coates."

"He must enjoy his work. I understand he likes to start early in the morning." Hayley's plan was to get in early tomorrow, too, before anyone else was at the office, and give him the card.

"He's always at the office by seven thirty a.m.," Brianna said. "That's why we don't drive in together. You and I should get an early start tomorrow too. Myra always takes all day, and she has a bunch of assistants."

"Eight o'clock?" Hayley said. That would allow her half an hour alone with Gordon.

"That's early enough for me," Brianna said cheerfully.

A short time later, she pulled off the highway into a vast parking lot already filling with Christmas shoppers. "We're here."

People were streaming into a sprawling barn-like building with multiple entrances. Brianna commandeered a shopping cart from the row outside and gestured to Hayley to do the same.

The shopping complex was comprised of dozens of individual antique and vintage stores, many of which were western style, collected under one soaring roof. The wide central corridor was lined with individual stores, and side branches led to other buildings and more shops. There were no pharmacies or department stores or modern boutiques, just acres and acres of the best of past eras, beautifully preserved. Hayley loved it.

"Oh. My. God," Hayley exclaimed. "All these antique and vintage items. I'm hyperventilating."

"Breathe," Brianna advised. "You're going to need a second wind to get through everything on offer here. So, what are we looking for?"

"I'm thinking deep jewel tones, muted, but rich—emerald and ruby with topaz accents for pops of brightness," Hayley said. "And a variety of textures."

"This is so exciting," Brianna said. "I can't wait to see this unfold."

"I can't wait to see what treasures we find," Hayley said. "We'll start with throws and cushions. We'll stay in the deep color palette for the downstairs with lighter and more romantic tones upstairs."

Last night, after leaving the bar, Hayley had drawn up a list of items to purchase using Blake's furniture as a base. Cushions, throws, decorative objects, wall hangings and paintings, vases. All needed to be carefully curated to create a cohesive look that exuded warmth and style. She'd only included the minimum essentials for each room. It wasn't about filling the house with everything a family would accumulate over years, but about creating a "look," just enough, and no more, to stimulate the imagination, so would-be buyers could visualize themselves living there.

"Blake said he would have his couch, dining table, and master bedroom furniture moved over today," Hayley said. As they moved slowly down the wide central corridor, she felt as if she'd died and gone to shopping heaven. "But we'll need some occasional furniture."

"Dad said to take photos and record prices and store details," Brianna said. "Then he or Blake will go through the list with you and place an order. If they can't deliver quickly enough, we'll send a truck to pick it up."

"Sounds good," Hayley said.

"Oh, I almost forgot." Brianna stopped and dug in her purse. She pulled out a square white envelope and handed it to Hayley, back side up.

"What's this?" For one heart-stopping moment Hayley thought that somehow she'd lost her mom's card and Brianna had picked it up. Then she turned it over and saw her name written in Brianna's exuberant scrawl.

"A Christmas card. If you're still here on Christmas eve, you're welcome to come to our place," Brianna said. "It's just family and a few close friends. Mom said it was okay."

"Thank you for inviting me," Hayley said, touched. "It's really nice of you, but I'll be spending the holiday back home with my mother."

"Totally understandable," Brianna said. "But the invitation is open if you change your mind."

"Do you live with your parents?" Hayley asked.

"I know what you're thinking," Brianna said. "At my

age, I should be on my own. I'm saving to buy my own place and, to be honest, I didn't expect to still be living in Sweetheart two years after college. I worked and traveled before I studied, so everything stretched out longer than I thought."

"It's all about the journey, though, right?" Hayley said. "How old are you, if you don't mind me asking?"

"I turned twenty-nine last month."

"I'll be thirty in March," Hayley said.

"We're almost twins," Brianna said, grinning.

Hayley laughed. *Twin cousins.* She opened her mouth to let the words out, but closed it again quickly.

"What?" Brianna said, smiling.

"Nothing. Oh, look." Hayley spotted a display of Native American artifacts and artisan products off the main corridor. "Those Navajo woven blankets make great throws." She chose a couple and placed them in her cart. "I may come back here."

Hayley and Brianna continued on down the side branch. It took an unexpected turn, and they ended up in another building that had been tacked on the original.

"It's too bad you weren't here for my birthday party," Brianna said. "I had a big bash with a band and dancing."

"How big?" Hayley asked.

"I invited sixty-five people."

"Half probably didn't show, right?" Hayley said, thinking of her experience with blanket invitations to social activities on Facebook.

Brianna glanced at her in surprise. "They all came, except for two or three who were either sick or out of town."

"You have sixty plus friends in—" She broke off, not wanting to say, "in this small town."

"In what?" Brianna asked, mystified.

"I mean, Sweetheart is a small town," Hayley said, embarrassed. "I don't see how you could know that many people to invite to a party."

"I didn't just invite friends my own age," Brianna said, smiling. "My friends' parents came too. People who have known me since I was a baby. And then there were my parents' close friends who are like aunts and uncles to me. I would have loved for my cousins from Vermont to come, but it was too close to Thanksgiving, and they had other plans." A shadow briefly crossed Brianna's face. "It's too bad we have so few relatives."

Again, Hayley had to stop herself from blurting out that she was Brianna's cousin. She wouldn't reveal the information until she'd spoken to Gordon. But, no matter what he said or did, before she left Sweetheart, she would tell Brianna the truth. They could keep in touch, and Brianna could visit Hayley and her mom in California.

"That sounds lovely," Hayley said. "Parties with a mix of age groups are the best."

"I agree," Brianna said. "Instead of presents, I asked everyone to bring a dish for a potluck dinner. It was a feast."

At a vintage bric-a-brac and housewares store, Hayley

picked up a set of copper-bottomed pots and ceramic canisters. She'd told Blake she would do a minimalist job but she couldn't help herself. She wanted the house to look amazing. "If your dad balks at any of this stuff, I'll buy it myself and take it home with me."

In the next store, Brianna found velvet throw pillows in deep sapphire blue. "What do you think?" she asked, holding them against the multi-colored throws.

"Perfect," Hayley said, adding several more in crimson. Up ahead, she spotted a display of linen and vintage lace draped over an old butter churn. "That gray linen, along with the ivory lace, would look amazing on Blake's four-poster."

An image of him, lying naked in the rumpled bedclothes, arms behind his head, popped into her mind.

"You okay?" Brianna asked. "You've gone all pink."

"It's a bit hot in here." Hayley unzipped her jacket and fanned herself.

"You're kidding me. This section has no heating." Brianna was bundled up in scarves and still had her knitted hat on. She gave Hayley a quizzical look. "Did you like his house on the Point?"

"Oh, yes. It's so beautiful, and the view over the lake and mountains is to die for." Hayley put the linen and lace in her cart. "I gathered from Blake that building it got him through a rough time after his engagement fell through. Not that it's any of my business," she added hastily. It wasn't, but she was interested in Brianna's reaction to Blake's engagement.

"Carrie was a nasty piece of work," Brianna said flatly. "She led him on for nearly two years and then flew the coop without warning. She dumped him by text once she'd gotten far enough away."

"Oh, my goodness, that's terrible," Hayley said.

"He was so trusting, he didn't even see it coming," Brianna said.

"Really? He seems so…cautious."

"Now he is," Brianna said. "She wasn't from around here. I don't think he'd met anyone like her before. None of us had. It's easy to be wise in hindsight but she had us all fooled for a while."

Hayley couldn't help but be curious about what kind of woman could make Blake so blinded by love that he lost his ability to judge her character. "What was she like?"

"Flashy. Exciting. Glamorous." Brianna shrugged. "She came across as everyone's best friend but in the end all she really cared about was herself."

"I bet she was hot." Blake was hot. It stood to reason he'd go for a woman who was his match. But he also had depth and character. She could never figure out why good men sometimes went for shallow women.

"Oh, she was hot all right," Brianna said darkly. "Hot enough to burn a guy." She moved along to a display of vintage earrings.

Hayley watched her hold a pair of dangly turquoise earrings up to her ear in front of a mirror, smile wistfully and put them back. "Sorry, I'm a sucker for jewelry. Need to keep my mind on what we're doing."

"They're pretty." Hayley held up a filigree gold earring. Her reflection in the mirror reminded her that she wasn't hot or flashy, more like the girl next door with polish. "So is he over her?"

Brianna nodded with a knowing smile. "Definitely."

Brianna wasn't hot or flashy either; she just had her own unique style. Gordon seemed to think that she and Blake would be a good match. Blake had disagreed, but could Brianna be carrying a torch for him?

"You and Blake must be close," she said. "Working together, family friends."

"He's the best," Brianna said warmly. "I don't know what I'd do without him, especially around the office. We've known each other since forever. He's practically part of the family."

"And in a romantic way?" Hayley inquired delicately.

"Blake and me? Oh, no, not at all." Brianna laughed. Then stopped abruptly. "Wait a minute. Where did you get that idea?"

Hayley hesitated. "Your father, actually, the night of the sleigh ride. Blake explained that Gordon would like you two to get together."

Brianna groaned. "Honestly, my dad is nuts. I love him dearly, but he's dreaming if he thinks Blake and I will ever get together again."

"Again?" Hayley repeated. "So you were a couple at one stage?"

"Years ago," Brianna said. "I was barely out of high school. Blake had just finished college and come back here to work. We were thrown together a lot, what with work and family, so going out on a date seemed a natural progression. Dad was pleased as punch, practically planning our wedding."

"But?" Hayley prompted.

"Zero chemistry." Brianna's hands flashed sideways, washing that notion right away. "We went out twice, just to be sure, but it was no use. The first—the only—time we kissed, it was like kissing one of my brothers. Ugh. Both of us knew immediately that we were making a mistake. Needless to say, that was the end. We're good friends, but that's all."

So Brianna was not an obstacle. That was a relief. "Is he seeing anyone else?" Hayley asked casually.

"He dates, but there's no one special." Brianna's jaw dropped. "Are you interested in him?" she squealed.

"Shh," Hayley cautioned. "No. Maybe. Well, yes, a little. But I don't think it could work out. I live so far away." And she couldn't encourage him as long as she was lying to him. God, why had she said anything to Brianna? Her cousin was adorable, but Hayley didn't know her well enough to trust that she wouldn't blurt it out without thinking. "Don't tell him, please. I would be so embarrassed."

"You would be perfect for him," Brianna said, undaunted.

"I've only known him a short time," Hayley protested.

"Yes, but sometimes you just know when it feels right," Brianna said. "That's what I think anyway."

"He invited me cross-country skiing after the spec home is done," Hayley said. "I'd really like to go but, well, we'll have to see." It depended on what the fallout was after she gave Gordon the Christmas card and everything was out in the open. "Promise you won't say anything to him about this."

"Don't worry, I won't," Brianna said, giving her a sideways hug. Then she pointed to a store farther along. "I'm going down there to buy some crocheted doilies for Christmas presents. Do you want to come? They're kind of retro cool."

"No, I'll be in that furniture store up ahead," Hayley said. "I see a side table that looks interesting. Meet me there when you're done."

Once Brianna was out of sight, Hayley doubled back to the jewelry counter. "I'll take those turquoise earrings." She tucked the small package in her purse, pleased with her purchase. She would enjoy imagining Brianna opening them on Christmas morning.

So, her cousin definitely wasn't interested in Blake. The way was open for Hayley to pursue a romantic relationship with him. Her smile faded. He'd been treated badly in the past. How interested would he still be after he found out the truth about her?

But, first things first. She still had the confrontation with Gordon ahead of her. She was here to connect with her uncle and reunite him with her mom. She needed to keep her mind on the reason she was here, not get distracted, even by a handsome builder who just might be The One.

Chapter Eleven

Friday morning, December 20

HAYLEY ARRIVED AT the office the next morning at seven thirty a.m. Sure enough, Gordon's car was the only one in the parking lot next to the office. The vehicles at the far end of the lot would be those owned by the guys who worked in the factory.

"Hello, anyone home?" Hayley knocked on the outer door and then pushed it open.

The lights were on, but the reception desk was unoccupied. Blake's office was dark too. Light showed beneath Gordon's door, which was ajar. Trembling with anticipation, she dipped her hand into her purse where her mom's card still sat in its envelope, now slightly dog-eared at the corners.

"Is someone there?" he called out.

"It's me, Hayley. Sorry to disturb you." She pushed open the door and peeked in. Gordon was at his computer, a spreadsheet of figures on the screen. "Getting an early start, I see."

His frown of concentration eased into a friendly smile as

he clicked his mouse and a screensaver came on. "What brings you out at this hour?"

"I'm an early riser too." She swallowed. Now that she was here, she was nervous about getting to the point of her visit. "Brianna and I are going to stage the spec home today. Figured, since I was up, I would just come along and wait for her."

"We sure appreciate you doing this," Gordon said. "Would you like a coffee?"

"That would be great. Can I get you a cup?" She glanced over her shoulder for a machine in reception, but there was none.

"It's in the kitchen. I could use a break." He rose and put a hand to his lower back and winced. "The doctor says I need to move more. I'm trying to get up once an hour, but sometimes I forget."

"Do you have back problems?" she asked.

"Just a little arthritis." He moved stiffly toward the door. "Coffee's in the staff room."

"My mom has arthritis in her hips," Hayley said as she followed him across the reception area. "She takes turmeric tablets."

"Do they help?" Moving more smoothly now, Gordon led the way down a short corridor to a small kitchen equipped with a microwave and a coffee maker.

"She thinks so," Hayley said. "She also does yoga to keep herself limber."

"Can't see myself in tights somehow." To illustrate, Gordon attempted a clumsy pose on one foot with arms and legs extended.

Startled at his antics, Hayley whooped with laughter. "Men usually wear shorts to class."

Her uncle cocked his head, his brows pulled together in a slight frown.

Hayley knew she had the same full-throated laugh as her mother, but this was the first time she'd unleashed it in her uncle's presence. "Something wrong?"

"No." He carried on scooping ground coffee into the top of the coffee maker. "You just reminded me of someone for a second."

She held her breath. It would be so much easier if he met her halfway by guessing she was a relation. "Who?"

"Just someone I used to know." Gordon had his back to her, busying himself with getting mugs down from the cupboard. The coffee maker made gurgling sounds. The silence between them started to feel awkward. "Haven't seen her for—gosh, decades."

She should just tell him who she was. Why was it so hard?

"I haven't seen my brother in nearly a year because he's working overseas for Doctors Without Borders," Hayley said. "I'd give anything to hear the sound of his laughter."

Gordon, still with his back to her, said gruffly, "Doesn't he get any vacation time?"

"I was out of town the last time he came home," she said.

"Brad got leave on short notice, but I was in Australia to source Indigenous artwork for a client. We missed seeing each other by a week. It was so disappointing."

"Brad, did you say?" Gordon turned, head tilted.

"Yes." Hayley became aware her heart was pounding. "He's a little over two years older than me."

Gordon only made a grunting sound of sympathy. "That's too bad you don't see him often."

"It's scary how easy it is to get out of touch," Hayley went on, twisting her hands together. "I have a friend who moved to the East Coast and hasn't seen her family in nearly ten years. I don't understand it myself. You'd think she would make a trip home once in a while. I don't think she even talks to her mom and dad on the phone very often."

She was rambling, sending out teasers, hoping he would pick up on what she was saying and share something of what he'd been through. But, either he wasn't getting the hint, or he was choosing not to. She came to an uneasy stop, not knowing what to say next.

"Maybe there's bad blood there." Gordon set cups on the table.

"Maybe," she agreed. "But maybe it's only a misunderstanding."

"Outsiders never know what really goes on in families." Gordon poured the coffee and changed the subject. "What did you think about the houses you've seen so far? Would any be suitable for your client?"

"They're all beautiful," she said. "But Blake's house on the point is amazing."

He passed her the carton of creamer. "Oh, well, Blake will never let that one go. He put his heart and soul into it."

"He told me the house isn't for sale, but at least I've seen a good example of a post and beam house." The ticking clock on the wall showed it was nearly eight a.m. Blake or Brianna might get here any moment. Now. She needed to act now. Who knew when she'd get her uncle alone again? Her palms turned clammy, and her heart picked up pace. She put her hand in her purse and felt for the envelope. "Gordon, there's something I've been wanting to tell you..."

Interested and alert, he focused on her with sharp blue eyes. Despite his thinning, graying hair and complaints about arthritic joints, he still looked vigorous in his midsixties. "What is it?"

Her heart pounded. She opened her mouth to speak.

The outer door creaked open and then shut. Footsteps. Walking across the wood floor, pausing.

Hayley's mouth clamped shut.

"Gordon?" Blake called. "Where are you?"

"In the kitchen," Gordon replied. "With Hayley." He turned to her. "What did you want to say?"

Hayley couldn't reply.

Blake came into the kitchen and got a mug from the cupboard. His gaze flicked from Hayley to Gordon and back to her.

173

"I…um…" She racked her brains, trying to think clearly. "Did you manage to get your furniture moved over to the spec home?"

"Sure did," Blake said. "I put the couch in front of the fireplace. Let me know if you want it moved."

"I'm sure that will be fine," Hayley said. Blake's expression was bland, but she could tell he'd picked up on her discomfort at speaking in front of him. Well, she couldn't help that. She was hardly going to blurt out the truth for the first time to Gordon in front of an audience.

Blake got himself a cup of coffee and headed for the door. "I'll be in your office when you're ready, Gordon. I presume you want to plan our strategy before John gets here."

"Be right there," Gordon said. He turned to Hayley. "You were going to tell me something?"

Hayley pulled the envelope from her purse. Before she could speak, the outer door banged, and Brianna entered, calling out. "Hayley? Blake, have you seen Hayley? Her car is in the lot."

Again, footsteps sounded on the floorboards, lighter, and with a sharper click, indicating women's boots.

Hayley thrust the envelope into Gordon's hands. "This is for you."

Then she turned and quickly went out. "Hey, Brianna. I'm ready. Let's get to work. We've got a lot to do."

BLAKE GLANCED UP as Gordon entered his office, carrying a white envelope. He passed the printouts of financial statements for the past five years across the desk to his boss. "Judging by our profit and loss statements and net worth, this is a very attractive company. Which Coates must have an inkling of, since he's sniffing around. Plus, he gets the added advantage of eliminating his competition."

When Gordon didn't reply, Blake glanced up. His boss seemed distracted, not surprising, given the meeting they had ahead of them. But, instead of getting down to work, he was studying the front of the envelope.

"What's that?" Blake asked.

"Looks like a Christmas card. Hayley gave it to me."

"Funny that she put a stamp and a return address on it but no delivery address," Blake said.

"Hm, yes, now that you mention it. Oh, well, I'll look at it later." Gordon set the card aside and straightened his glasses. "Back to business. As far as I'm concerned, today is just a fact-finding mission, but Coates might be coming here with an offer."

"He'll lowball you, for sure, just to test the waters," Blake said. "If this goes any further than today, you should think about bringing Aiden in for a legal perspective. In fact, maybe Aiden should be here now, so we don't get caught off guard."

"Not yet. I want to keep this low-key for now," Gordon said. "Doesn't do to look like I'm eager to start negotiations."

From the reception area came the sound of the outer door opening and closing. "Hello?" Coates called a moment later.

Blake and Gordon exchanged a glance. Blake rose to go bring Coates in, then he reached across the desk to grip Gordon's forearm. "I've got your back," he said in a low voice. "I'm your second pair of ears and eyes. Don't commit to anything and I mean nothing. Listen to his offer and tell him you need time to think about it." He paused. "Are you ready?"

Gordon nodded. "Show him in."

Blake rose and opened the door. "John, good to see you."

John Coates brought in the scent of cold and snow. The first few words were all about the weather and the roads. A round of hearty handshakes and smiles and they all sat down again.

For the next half hour, Coates did most of the talking, throwing around vague figures to gauge their response. Blake did most of the replying and questioning. Gordon listened and put in a few words now and then. Coates attempted to negotiate, but Blake blocked him at every turn.

Finally, Coates could see that he wasn't going to get any further today. He drew a sheet of paper from his briefcase and laid it in front of Gordon. "Here is my best offer. I don't think anyone else would beat it. We could wrangle all day long about staff and assets, but it comes down to one thing. I want to buy your company. I'm willing to make it worth your while. In exchange for a price that is more than fair, I will accept no conditions in terms of retaining staff. Those personnel I do decide to keep, I reserve the right to renegotiate their current contracts."

Gordon looked at the offer. His eyebrows rose. He passed it to Blake. Blake saw it and a hot rush of adrenaline flooded his system. The offer was more than generous; it was unbelievably extravagant.

"Gentlemen." John Coates rose, buttoned his suit jacket over his trim stomach, and offered his hand first to Gordon and then to Blake. "My offer is good until close of business on Christmas eve. Think about it and let me know."

"We'll be in touch," Gordon said, half rising to shake before subsiding into his chair. His glasses were perched on top of his head, the printed sheet Coates had given him still in his hand. He looked dazed.

Blake got to his feet too. "I'll see you out. Be right back, Gordon."

His spirits were heavy as he walked Coates out to the reception area and to the door. Gordon was going to accept; he'd be crazy not to.

"Thanks for coming by, John." Blake shook his hand again. "I know Gordon will give your offer all due consideration."

"What will you advise him?" Coates asked, putting on his overcoat.

"There's a lot to discuss," Blake said. "In the end, it's his decision."

"Yes, but I'm asking you," Coates persisted. "In his place, what would you do?"

"I would do what's best for the company," Blake said, giving nothing away of the tumultuous emotions he was experiencing.

John Coates laughed. "Not going to get anything out of you, am I?"

"Nope."

"Not even if I tell you that I would keep you on as manager?"

Blake smiled. "Not even then."

"You have shares in the company?" Coates asked.

"I do." Blake could see where this was going. It might make another man feel buoyant. Not him. He wanted company ownership to remain in Sweetheart, with Gordon at the helm. Or himself. Anything but having John Coates suck the life and soul out of the family-run business.

"I floated Coates Construction on the stock market earlier this year," Coates went on. "Once Sweetheart Log Homes is under our umbrella, your stocks will double, maybe triple, in value."

"Good to know." Blake stepped back and shut the door before Coates could say anything else. He muttered to himself, "Money isn't everything."

STAGING A HOUSE was a huge job, one that required all Hayley's physical energy and mental concentration. When she and Brianna arrived at the spec home, Blake's furniture was already there and in position. A delivery truck got there soon after, and the men brought in beds, side tables, and miscellaneous small pieces of furniture and lamps that she and Brianna had bought the day before.

Dressed in yoga pants, a long-sleeved T-shirt, and sneakers, Hayley was ready to work. She directed the men where to place the heavy items and carried what she could manage. There was so much to focus on—arranging furniture, making up beds, placing throw pillows, laying rugs, positioning small plants and artful decorations, and on and on.

Upstairs, Hayley walked from room to room. Blake's king-size four-poster was in the master, a queen in the guest room, bunk beds in the third room, but there was nothing for the fourth bedroom. Or was it a storage room? It was quite small. Maybe she could find a small couch and bookshelf and turn it into a reading room.

Back in the master, boxes of linens were stacked in a corner. She quickly made up the bed, using a steamer she'd purchased at the hardware store to smooth out the sheets. A tumble of pillows, a drape of fabric over the windows to tie in the color scheme, lamps on the side tables, a framed oil painting of wildflowers over the bed, a few ornaments, and voilà!

In the en suite, she hung fluffy new towels, placed a candle next to a small succulent in an earthenware pot. She moved quickly and efficiently and went on to the next room, working on automatic pilot, a bundle of nerves as her mind busily wondered what Gordon was thinking. Had he read the card? Of course, he had, why wouldn't he? It took only a moment to open and look at. So why hadn't he called? Every now and then she checked her phone but there were no messages. Maybe he'd called her mother directly. But if he had, then her mom would call her right away, and she hadn't. So what was going on?

When she was done upstairs, she went back downstairs to set up the living room.

"I can't believe how many pillows there are," Brianna commented as she carried an armload upstairs. "There must be dozens."

"Forty-two to be precise," Hayley said, draping a throw over the back of the leather couch and tucking the end behind a cluster of velvet pillows. Having done that, she arranged smaller items around the room—photo frames, scented candles, more succulents in pots, and sets of wooden letters that spelled out *home* and *hearth*.

With the open house tomorrow, they had no time for breaks. Hayley had placed an open bag of trail mix on the kitchen counter, along with bottles of water. Stopping to grab a handful of nuts and a drink, she again checked her phone for missed calls and messages. Nothing from Gordon. She couldn't stand the suspense. Had he even opened her mother's card yet? Maybe not. He had the meeting with John Coates, so he would be busy during the morning, and who knew what developments had flowed on from that encounter. She tucked her phone back in her pocket and carried on. Best to keep busy.

She and Brianna were run off their feet all day long. Angus arrived and helped them position furniture, hang pictures, and cart away the packing material. By five thirty, Hayley was damp with perspiration, and her arms and legs were sore from carrying. She stopped, hands on hips, and looked around, pleased with their efforts. The empty log house had been transformed into a display home. "We're done for now."

"It looks fabulous," Brianna said, standing back to take in the open-plan living room, dining area, and kitchen.

"Blake's furniture works well," Hayley acknowledged.

"Yes, but it's everything else, the colors, the textures, the details," Brianna said. "I never could have done anything this good on my own."

"I couldn't have done it without your help." Hayley smiled at her. "I'll come back first thing in the morning with fresh flowers for the entryway and the living room and to double check everything's in place. For now, I'll take some photographs to show your dad and Blake."

Brianna grabbed an empty box. "I'll start picking up the odds and ends of trash. Then let's get out of here."

It was after six o'clock by the time she and Brianna got back to the office. With some trepidation, Hayley followed Brianna inside. Blake was in his office; she could hear him talking on his phone. Her gaze scanned the long loops of Christmas cards strung along the wall. Her heart sank when she saw that her mother's card wasn't there. Then lifted again at the thought that maybe Gordon was keeping it for himself, propped on his desk.

Brianna knocked on her father's door and went in. "We finished the staging. How did it go with John Coates?"

"I'll tell you about it later," Gordon said. "How did the staging go?"

"The house looks fabulous," Brianna said. "Hayley's got photos."

Hayley had hung back, but now she made her way to Gordon's office. She quickly scanned his desk and bookshelves but couldn't see the card anywhere. "Hey," she said with a shy smile for her uncle and took the proffered chair.

Gordon nodded at her, his genial expression giving her no clue as to whether he'd even looked at her card. "Did everything come that you ordered?"

"Yes," Hayley said and brought out her phone. Of course he wasn't going to start talking about her mom right now. He was at work. Business came first. She brought up the gallery and passed her phone across the desk. "Scroll right. The rooms aren't in any particular order, but you'll get the idea."

Blake appeared in the doorway. "I see the decorators have returned." He came in and looked over Gordon's shoulder at the photos. "Oh, wow."

As Blake and Gordon flicked through the photos, they nodded approvingly and made the occasional comment. Hayley explained her vision for a rustic, but comfortable, aesthetic, with a few exotic items like Moroccan carpets that fit with the color scheme and added an extra dimension, while blending in with the western look, resulting in a warm, inviting home.

"Usually I go for a minimalist look," Hayley said. "But the home is so large, and the logs such a dominant feature, I think we can get away with the extra touches that give a feeling of comfort and coziness."

When they came to the end of the photo gallery, Blake was visibly impressed. "This is excellent."

"In two days, you shopped for, and staged, the entire house," Gordon said. "That's fast work."

"My head was spinning!" Brianna chimed in. "Hayley has so much energy and so many ideas."

"It's what I do." She smiled, pleased at their approval. Then had to confess. "The small room at the end of the hallway isn't decorated. From the plans, I wasn't sure if it was a bedroom or a storage room."

"It could be a fourth bedroom or an office," Blake said. "We'll find something for it."

"This was a lot of work," Gordon said. "Hayley, make sure you invoice us for your time."

"Oh, no, that's okay." She waved that away. "I'll put the photos on my website, if that's okay, and consider it a fair exchange."

"You're welcome to use them," Gordon said. "But I won't hear of you not getting paid."

Hayley shrugged, not wanting to argue the point. "You'll probably want to keep the furnishings for future staging. I have a small warehouse at home with my stock. Do you have any storage space?"

"Not set aside for furniture," Gordon said. "It's an investment we don't normally take on."

"Maybe we should," Blake said. "We could do our own staging in the future."

Gordon gave him a look. "The future is what I'm pondering."

"Furnishings are an asset, adding to the value of the company's holdings," Blake said.

"Instant depreciation," Gordon countered. A faint undercurrent of tension hummed between the two men.

"It's a departure from your current procedure," Hayley acknowledged to Gordon. "Whatever you don't want, I'll buy from you. I can always use new furnishings. I don't want you to be stuck with anything unwanted on my account."

"She can't be more fair than that," Blake said. "Right, Gordon?"

"We'll figure it out," Gordon said to Hayley. "You've done us a big enough favor already."

"Okay," she said then hesitated. The issue had been resolved, yet nobody moved or said anything. Brianna seemed to be waiting to talk to her father. Blake wasn't budging either. Okay, that was her cue to leave. She would have to wait a little longer to find out what Gordon's reaction was to her mother's card.

And then she saw it, peeking out from beneath a pile of documents. The back was facing up. The seal hadn't been broken! All day she'd been wondering and worrying about Gordon's reaction, and he hadn't even opened it. Hiding the tumult of emotions running through her, she picked up her phone and touched Brianna's shoulder. "See you tomorrow morning."

Brianna smiled up at her. "Cool."

"I appreciate your efforts, Hayley," her uncle said. "I'll be in touch."

From his genial, bland expression, she had no clue whether he'd even given the card a second thought. "Call me if you want to talk further…about anything," she hinted.

Blake started to rise to walk her out. She raised a hand to stop him. "I know my way by now. See you soon."

She hurried out, wanting to get away before anyone noticed she was upset and wondered why. Hopefully, by tomorrow, this would all be over. Gordon would have opened the card, she would have talked to him about her mom, and everything would be okay. Then she could finally explain to Blake what she was doing here. They could go skiing and really talk. Beyond that, she couldn't even think. She only hoped that if Blake was seriously interested in her, they could somehow find a way to make their paths in life join together.

BLAKE SANK BACK into his seat, but his gaze followed Hayley as she left. He knew Brianna would want to talk to her father about Coates's offer, and he didn't want to miss that conversation, but he also wanted to speak to Hayley. The way her gaze had homed in on the unopened card and then flicked to Gordon had made him wonder. Then her suggestion that Gordon call her, about "anything" caused his mind to whir. In fact, the card had been bothering him all day. The fact that it was stamped, with a return address but no delivery address, and the way she'd given it to Gordon privately was very strange. Blake felt as if the secret she was hiding was tantalizingly within reach.

"Tell me about Coates's offer," Brianna said. "I'm dying to hear what happened."

Gordon took the piece of paper from the folder and passed it to her.

Brianna's eyes went wide. "Oh, my God. We can all retire on that."

"I have no interest in retiring," Blake said.

"It's far more than I expected," Gordon said. "I know what Anita will say. Take the money and run."

"There's got to be a catch," Brianna said, now perusing the fine print.

"There is," Blake said. "Fifty percent of our staff would be let go. Before Christmas. No bonus, no payout. Just gone."

"Dad, you're not seriously considering doing that," Brianna said, shocked. "The guys have worked so hard for you, most of them for many years."

"With this kind of money I could give the guys a payout." Gordon sounded upbeat, as if tempted by the thought that he could retire in comfort and do right by his employees. "I want to talk it over with your mother. Then I need to sleep on it." He got slowly to his feet and gathered up the annual report and the other papers Coates had left.

"Hang on a second, please, Dad," Brianna said. "There's something else I want to speak to you about."

"Can we talk about it at home?" Gordon said. "It's been a long day, and your mother will be waiting with dinner for us."

"I want Blake to be here," she said. "Anyway, I'm not going home right away. This shouldn't take long, but it has to be now."

Blake exchanged a glance with Gordon and shrugged, mystified.

Gordon resumed his seat. "What is it?"

"You need to stop thinking that Blake and I will ever be a couple," Brianna said. "It'll never happen. You're giving people the wrong impression."

Oh, boy. Blake dragged a hand through his hair and leaned back in his chair. This issue needed to be addressed, but Brianna's timing sucked.

"A couple?" Gordon said, frowning. "I don't think I've used that precise term. Who have I given that impression to?"

"Hayley, for one," Brianna said. "At the sleigh ride. She mentioned it yesterday when we were shopping."

"Well, what about it?" Gordon said. "Why should it bother her?"

Blake listened attentively for Brianna's reply. Had Hayley indicated she'd be disappointed to think he was destined for Brianna?

"I'm not going to discuss Hayley's feelings, whatever they might be," Brianna said. "But it's misleading. Right, Blake?"

Blake nodded, and then gave Gordon an apologetic shrug. "I tried to tell you, sir."

"So have I." Brianna fixed her father with a stern look, so like Gordon's own when he was asserting his authority, that Blake had to suppress a smile. "Blake and I, together, that's never going to happen."

"But you two are so fond of each other." Gordon also looked to Blake for affirmation. "Right?"

"I am very fond of Brianna," Blake said carefully. "But fond isn't the same as love."

"Well, well." Gordon looked as if he'd aged five years. "I was hoping that one day you two would run the business together."

"I *would* like to run the business," Blake said, seizing the opportunity to let his desires be known. "I was hoping you wouldn't retire for another few years so I could get the money together. Even if I waited ten years, I could never match what Coates is offering, but you know how hard I'm willing to work. Given a chance to buy you out, I would redouble my efforts. If we talked it over, I'm sure we could come to some mutually beneficial agreement. Designing and building log homes, running this business, and continuing your legacy, is all I've ever wanted."

In a few sentences, he laid bare his hopes, dreams, and plans. The company's future, his future, whatever he might, or might not, have going with Hayley. Everything was up in the air. He'd never felt so exposed in his life, as if he was spinning into the ether without a safety net.

"Well, I don't want to stay at this job forever," Brianna said, jumping in before her father could reply to Blake. "I told you that when I started, but you keep forgetting, or hoping I'll change my mind. I won't. If you sell to Coates, I'll be out of here. I'm not going to work for that man."

"You really don't love Blake?" Gordon replied, apparently still unable to get past that painful truth.

And, just like that, they were back to relationships. Blake rubbed his temples. He'd put all his cards on the table about the business, and Gordon had swept them aside. Had he even heard what he'd said?

"I'm sorry to disappoint you, Dad." A pained expression twisted her features. "I've been seeing Angus."

"Angus from the factory?" Gordon said, his voice rising.

"Blake started in the mill," Brianna pointed out quickly. "Give him a chance, like you gave Blake."

"That was different," Gordon said. "Blake has proved himself."

"Angus is taking night school classes in business," Blake said. "He's a smart dude."

"What about you?" Gordon asked, turning back to Blake. "Do you have a woman in your life? I mean someone you're serious about?"

"There is someone I'm interested in," he said carefully. "But it's complicated, and she doesn't know it herself, so I'd rather not talk about it."

"This is all too much right now," Gordon said, agitated. "I've got other things to think about." When Brianna started to object, he held up a hand. "Don't worry, I've gotten the message about you and Blake." He got slowly to his feet and gathered up all his documents: the company's finances, Coates's offer—Hayley's card—and put them inside his briefcase. "I'll see you at home, Brianna. Blake, we'll talk soon."

Blake and Brianna listened to his footsteps cross the reception area. The other door opened. Then shut.

"That went well," Brianna said. "Not."

"He accepted the situation with us," Blake said. "It will take him a while to like it, but he wants you to be happy, so, in the end, he'll accept Angus too."

"I hope you're right." Brianna started to rise. "I'll get going too. I'm meeting Angus at the tavern."

"Have you got another minute to chat?" Blake said. "I'm just a little curious about that card Hayley gave him. He took it home."

"So?" Brianna said.

"Cards that come to the business address, you hang up in the reception area," he reminded her.

"He probably didn't even notice it was with his papers," Brianna said. "What difference does it make?"

"It's just that…" Blake struggled to put into words the idea that was growing in his mind. "I don't think she wrote it. There's a return address from California on it. And a stamp."

"Hayley is from California," Brianna said with a shrug.

"Why would she give a total stranger a Christmas card in the first place?" Blake asked. "She's barely spent any time with Gordon."

"Goodwill gesture toward a business acquaintance?" Brianna hazarded a guess.

"Why put her return address and a stamp on the envelope if she was going to give it to him by hand?" Blake persisted.

"So he has her address for future reference?" Brianna suggested.

"She's already given us her business card," Blake said. "Which, I noted, is different from the address on the card."

"So?" Brianna said. "It must be her home address."

"Think about it. Would she really have bought a card in advance, gone to the trouble of addressing and stamping it, and then not mail it?" Blake said. "She didn't even know your father before she came here. None of it makes sense."

"Okay, it is a bit odd," Brianna said. "Maybe the card has nothing to do with her at all. Maybe it fell out of the mailman's bag on the ground outside and she simply found it and handed it to Dad. She was here well before us this morning."

"The stamp wasn't cancelled by the post office so it didn't come via the mailman," Blake said. "And why did she come in so early if not to see your father alone? They were deep in conversation when I arrived."

"I give up." Brianna threw up her hands. "You don't still think she's working for Coates, do you?"

"No, I'm sure she's not," Blake said. "I could be wrong, but what if the card is from his long-lost sister, Joyce?"

"His sister! But how would Hayley know—" Brianna

began. "Oh! Does that mean she's…Dad's niece?"

Blake nodded. "And your cousin."

"My cousin." Brianna stared at him and then scrambled for her phone. "Oh, my god. I'm going to call her right now."

"Whoa, not so fast. We don't know for sure that she's related," Blake said. "Whatever is going on, it's not really about Hayley. Gordon and his sister had a bad falling out years ago. This is between them. Let's see how this plays out before we confront Hayley."

"Confront her?" Brianna repeated. "What are you talking about? I'm going to welcome her to the family."

"I still think you should wait," Blake counseled. "Talk to your dad about it first. See what his feelings are before you barrel ahead with Hayley. We don't even know what's in the card. It's possible his sister isn't reaching out in a positive way. She could be dredging up old grievances."

"Knowing Hayley, I don't believe it."

"I admit, it seems unlikely, but still…"

"I don't care." Brianna pulled out her phone and dialed. "Whatever is wrong between Dad and his sister doesn't mean that Hayley and I can't be friends." She listened a moment and then clicked the phone off without leaving a message. "Gone to voice mail."

"Let's call it a night," Blake said. "I need to be up early. I imagine Hayley will want a restful evening herself."

"Are you kidding?" Brianna said. "She's probably biting

her nails right now, wondering when Dad's going to open the card and, when he does, what will be going through his mind. I'm going to call him."

"He'll still be driving," Blake said. "He doesn't like to use hands free. Wait till you get home."

"Why are you stalling me on this? Don't you want to know the truth?" Brianna said. "If Hayley is my cousin and her mom is trying to make contact with my dad, then this is huge for our family."

Blake threw up his hands. "Do what you want."

Typically perverse, having gotten her way, Brianna now took the opposite approach. "No, I'll wait and talk to Dad in person. Right now, Angus is waiting for me. But I will get to the bottom of this."

She gave Blake a quick, excited hug. "This is a good thing, you'll see. Hayley is wonderful. I'll bet her mom is too. Oh, and she has a brother! Another cousin. This is fantastic!"

When Blake didn't say anything, her smile faded. "What's wrong? Are you okay?"

"Sure, I'm fine. This is great news for your family." From somewhere, he found a smile.

After Brianna left, Blake got his coat and went out, locking up behind him. Rebel frisked through the abandoned parking lot, joyful at being outdoors after a long afternoon cooped up. Blake did a quick circuit of the factory and made sure all the doors and windows were secure.

Driving home, his thoughts went over everything that had happened that day. Coates's offer hung over his head like an ax waiting to drop on his career, but what was really bothering him was Hayley. If she was Gordon's niece, then did that mean that everything Blake had done with her this past week was a lie? Was there even a client? She seemed genuinely interested in log homes, but had that really been her purpose in coming to town, or was it solely to meet her uncle? Even staging the spec home…was that a coup for her portfolio, or had she seized the opportunity as a way to butter Gordon up for her mom's sake? How much of what she'd said to him about anything was real? If she'd lied about having a client she could have lied about anything, or everything. He'd flattered himself that she was attracted to him, but maybe her sole aim had been to get into her uncle's good books.

For months before Carrie left him, she'd acted as though nothing was wrong between them, giving no clue that she was going to break off their engagement. She'd let him go on planning their future together and, all the while, she'd been getting her life as a single person in order. She'd gone to Denver, supposedly to visit a college friend, found a job, and rented an apartment, all without telling him. With everything in place, she was able to make a quick getaway and not have to deal with the emotional fallout from her leaving.

Likewise, Hayley had snuck under his radar with her sweet smile and her confidences and hint of vulnerability, and all the while she'd told him a pack of lies. She'd probably never been interested in him at all. He thought of how he'd been about to kiss her on the sleigh ride before she'd turned away and he flinched at the memory. What a fool he'd been.

Chapter Twelve

Friday evening, December 20

HAYLEY DROVE BACK into town in turmoil. Gordon had had the card all day and hadn't read it. How much longer was this going to drag on? To be fair, he'd been preoccupied with his meeting with John Coates and all the consequences of deciding whether or not to sell his business.

As she drove, the negative thoughts gave way to more positive ones. At least she'd finally given him the card, a huge weight off her shoulders. It would get opened, one way or another, very soon. That things were finally coming to a head buoyed her. Gordon was a kind and generous man. Once he'd read her mom's card, surely Joyce would be reunited with her long-lost brother.

Brianna called her phone just as she turned onto Swan Street. Hayley was tempted to pick up, but she was driving, so she let it go. It was probably something about the spec home. She would call her back later.

First, she wanted to stop at Outdoor Adventures to rent a pair of cross-country skis. The store was brightly lit, warm, and welcoming. Pop renditions of Christmas carols played over the sound system, the potbellied stove in the corner blasted out hot air, and, seated next to it on a rough-hewn wooden bench softened with cushions, a young couple leafed through a colorful brochure on winter adventure tours.

Hayley walked further into the store. Posters depicting heli-skiing, snowboarding, and white-water kayaking papered the walls above shelves laden with ski and snowboard paraphernalia and accessories. At the back of the store, she recognized Garrett Starr, in a blue plaid shirt and jeans, discussing the relative merits of different snowboards with a pair of teenage boys.

Hayley gravitated to the racks of winter clothing and flicked through the ski jackets. Her red jacket would do, but why not get something more suitable, especially if she might be skiing more in the future? She could envision spending every Christmas in Sweetheart, or maybe every second Christmas. Gordon and Anita might enjoy coming out to California for the holidays some years, to spend them with her, Mom, and Brad.

Thoughts of Brad brought forth a sigh. He still hadn't called her back. Well, she wouldn't bother him again. He would have to be next to pick up the phone.

She tried on a bright blue jacket and checked herself in the mirror at the end of the clothes rack. It fit perfectly, felt comfortable, and she liked the look. Sold.

The boys departed, each with a brand-new snowboard

tucked under their arms. Garrett wandered over to Hayley. "You're Hayley, right? We met at my parents' open house."

"That's right," she said. "Nice to see you again."

"That's a great brand," he said, nodding at the jacket. "Let me know if you need any help."

"I'm looking for a few things for cross-country skiing," she said. "I'll take this jacket. I'll also need a pair of gloves and a beanie."

"The gloves are over here." Carrying the jacket for her, he led the way to the shelf of gloves. "Blake told me he was taking you up to Blacktail this weekend."

"That's the plan," she said following him. "I understand you and Blake have been friends since childhood."

"Yep. We go way back." Garrett passed her a pair of silver and purple insulated gloves. "Try these for size."

She tried to slip one on, but it was too small. "Is there a size up?"

He handed her another pair. "Have you found a log house to buy yet?"

"Not yet," she said. "I love the one Blake built for himself, but he doesn't want to let it go."

"No way. He loves that house," Garret said. "How are those gloves?"

"Perfect. I don't suppose you have them in blue to match the jacket?"

"Let's see." Garrett dug through the row of gloves. "Here we go. Right size too." He waited while she tried them on just to make sure. "So, are you going to stick around?"

Startled, Hayley glanced up. "I'm not sure what you mean."

"I mean Blake is a good guy. He doesn't need another woman messing with his head." Garrett's manner was calm, not aggressive, but his words were very blunt in defense of his friend.

"If you're talking about his ex-fiancée," Hayley said stiffly. "I wouldn't do what she did to my worst enemy."

"Okay, sorry. I shouldn't have said anything. It's none of my business." Garrett moved toward the stacks of folded knitted caps. "Blue?"

"What has Blake said?" Hayley asked, following him. "Does he think I'm messing with him?" She hadn't told him everything and he seemed to sense that. For a man who might justifiably have trust issues, it wouldn't be surprising if he questioned her intentions.

"He hasn't said so, but you'll forgive me for being cautious on his behalf," Garrett said. "He's tough, but he's also got a vulnerable side. I wouldn't like to see him get hurt again."

"I don't want to hurt anyone, least of all Blake." But Hayley could see that she might do so inadvertently. She took off her own hat and tried on the beanie. It was snug and warm. "Is he still not over his ex?"

"No, the wound has healed. But scars don't fade overnight." Garrett hesitated and then let loose with what had obviously bothered him for a long time. "Carrie could be very warm and charming, but she was a narcissist. All she cared about was herself and what she wanted."

"How awful for Blake," Hayley murmured a trifle guiltily. "How did they meet?"

"She came one summer for the cherry harvest," Garrett said. "They met at our orchard, and he fell for her. She was fun and outgoing but she'd had a troubled childhood, which Blake could relate to. Because people had given him a break, he gave her more trust than she deserved. After picking was over, he helped her get another job in town, find better accommodations, and he introduced her to all his friends. Being with him gave her credence around town that she wouldn't have had otherwise."

"What happened?" Hayley asked.

"Everything seemed to be going great but eventually cracks appeared in her façade and it became clear she had issues," Garrett said. "Blake ignored the warning signs because he was infatuated. She spent every cent she earned on clothes, makeup, a new car. He ended up paying her rent for her because she'd blown all her money. But he was in love, and he thought she was too. Then he asked her to marry him. That was the beginning of the end."

"She wasn't serious about him?" Hayley's heart wrenched imagining Blake's heartbreak.

"Not at all." Garrett snorted. "She was stringing him along, using him, plain and simple. One morning he woke up, and she was gone, poof, without a word."

"How awful," Hayley said.

"He hasn't let his guard down for a woman in two years until you came along," Garrett said. "He doesn't say a lot, but I can tell he really likes you. It isn't any of my business, but he's my best friend, so I'm going to say it anyway. Do not lie to him. Do not say you're going to stick around if you have no intention of doing so."

"I have no intention of hurting him," Hayley murmured. But she had lied to him about her reasons for being in Montana and she hated that. If only she'd confided in him from the beginning. Instead, his suspicions of her had made her go to greater lengths to hide her true purpose. Now she felt sick at the thought of facing Blake once he knew everything.

As for sticking around... It was fun to toy with the idea of living in Sweetheart, but would she really give up her life and her business in California? Or had the appeal of the small town and falling for Blake clouded her vision? All of a sudden, she wasn't sure.

"I'd better go," she said. "Did Blake reserve me a pair of skis? I can take them now."

"He picked them up the other day," Garrett said.

"Please add the cost to my bill and credit Blake." Knowing what Carrie had done to him, there was no way she wanted him to think she would take advantage of his generosity.

Garrett processed her credit card and bagged her purchases. "Sorry if I sounded harsh. I love that guy like a brother."

Hayley gave Garrett a lopsided smile. "For what it's worth, I like him too. I mean, really like him."

As in, love. And what was she going to do about it?

Back at the hotel, she ordered room service, and opened a half bottle of wine from the mini bar. With her new ski jacket and accessories spread out on the bed, she tried Brianna's number. No answer.

No messages from Gordon either.

Or Blake.

It was only an hour and a half since she'd left the three of them at the office, but the radio silence was getting to her. What if things didn't go the way she was hoping? What if the others had stayed behind to talk about her? Would Gordon open the card in the presence of Brianna and Blake? Would they discuss her mom and her? Maybe she should have said something to Gordon, but if he hadn't read the card, it was hard to know what to say.

Her dinner came, and she ate, cross-legged on the bed, staring blankly at a game show on the TV. Judging by the strings of cards lining the Sweetheart Log Homes office, they must receive dozens and dozens. No doubt there were lots more at his home. What if, to him, it was just another card? What if he didn't even open it? Of course he would open it. If not, Brianna or Anita would. And then everything would be out in the open.

Once Gordon and his family knew, then Blake would know.

Now that she'd handed on the card, she should tell Blake herself why she was here, rather than let him find out secondhand. Given his history with Carrie, she was probably the last person he would want to date, but suddenly she couldn't wait any longer to talk to him. To reassure him that she'd never intended to deceive him, and reassure herself that he cared enough not to reject her, even though he had every right to.

Pulling on her coat and boots, she went back out into the snowy night. A few minutes later, she drew up in Blake's driveway. Rebel heard her car and started barking like crazy. Then the front door opened, spilling golden light across the snow.

Blake stood in the doorway.

"QUIET, REBEL," BLAKE told his barking dog and opened the front door.

Hayley's car was in his driveway. Seeing him, she turned off the motor. Through the windshield, he could see her eyes shut briefly, and then she straightened her shoulders and got out of the car.

A moment ago, he had been slumped in front of a hockey game on TV that he wasn't really watching, gloomily mulling over the fact that once again he'd fallen for a woman who was going to end up hurting him. He couldn't be sure about the significance of that Christmas card but it was clear that Hayley was keeping secrets, from him and from everyone. Moreover, she was going to return to California in a few days. The anticipation of losing her was hitting him all the harder because of what had happened with Carrie. Although by the time Carrie had done her worst, he'd realized that what he'd thought was love had only been infatuation.

But Hayley was different, more genuine. Or so he'd thought. What he felt for her was different, more real and lasting. But hadn't he thought that about Carrie at first too? He groaned, no longer sure what he thought or felt. Would Hayley ever tell him the whole truth? Had she gotten whatever it was that she came here for? And if she had, did that mean that once she left she wouldn't ever come back? Hayley hadn't damaged his pride and taken his money like Carrie had but she'd stolen something much more precious—his heart.

Now she was getting out of her car and walking toward him. A blue knit cap sat atop her shiny blonde hair, and she wore a blue jacket over her jeans and boots. Rebel bounded toward her and danced around her legs, barking joyously. She stopped to pet him and then straightened.

"Are you busy?" she asked.

A reasonable question. Any other Friday night, he might

be found at the tavern having a brew or two with his pals. Instead, he was watching the idiot box with his dog. Two pairs of skis stood in the corner of the living room, ready for an expedition that he didn't even want to go on any longer.

"I was about to head out," he lied.

"Can I come in?" she said. "Just for a minute. I need to talk to you."

"All right." Blake stepped back to let her in and caught a wave of cold air, snow, and the scent of her perfume, that took him back to a more innocent time a mere few days ago. She followed him around a half wall into the living room. He switched off the TV. "Have a seat. Do you want a beer?"

"No, thanks." Hayley perched on the edge of the sofa, took off her hat and gloves, then clasped her hands tightly together above her knees.

Blake sat back in his chair, noting the nervous darts of her gaze, the way her fingers clutched each other. "What did you want to talk about?"

Her lips pressed together, and she frowned as if searching for the right words. "The first thing I need to do is apologize to you."

"For?" he asked. Maybe now she was finally going to come clean about her real reason for coming to Sweetheart. An apology might not be enough, but he wanted to hear what she had to say.

"I…I never meant to mislead you or anyone," she said, speaking quickly. "I didn't have a big plan when I came to

Sweetheart other than giving Gordon that Christmas card."

"Maybe you should start with the card," Blake said. "Who is it from? Not you, I take it."

"No, it's from my mother." She took a deep breath, her hands sandwiched between her knees. "She is Gordon's sister. I'm his niece."

Blake nodded, took a swig of beer.

"You don't look surprised," she said.

"I guessed."

"When?"

"Today."

"I'm really, really sorry for not telling you who I was from the beginning." She swallowed, looking as if she was ready to burst into tears. "I had good reasons. At least, they seemed reasonable to me."

"It's easier to transgress and apologize later," he said dryly.

"I didn't mean to hurt you."

"What makes you think you could?" he said, hoping she wouldn't see the flash of pain that ripped through him.

"Not hurt," she amended quickly. "We haven't known each other that long."

Long enough for him to fall hard for her. "Why didn't you say anything?"

"I wanted to but I couldn't, not until I'd spoken to Gordon." Her eyes pleaded with him to understand.

And he did to a certain extent but her behavior had

dredged up old feelings of his time with Carrie and those couldn't be lightly brushed aside. "I trusted you. I let you in. I thought you were real. I thought the connection between us was real."

"It is real," she said desperately. "It was. It can be again."

"How can it be real when it's based on a lie?" he demanded. If she could spin a believable lie about a client that easily then what other lies might she tell him in the future? "I take it there's no client."

"No." Hayley's hands lifted and then fell helplessly. "My interest in log homes is genuine."

"Now it is, maybe," he said. "But not when you first came."

"No," she admitted. "I gained that interest partly thanks to you. I appreciate the time you spent with me and it won't be wasted, I guarantee. There aren't a lot of log homes in Southern California, but there are in the northern part of the state. I don't mind traveling for work."

"Gordon is a standup guy," Blake went on, venting on his boss's behalf. "Family is everything to him. He would have welcomed you with open arms. But you pretended to him, too."

"Now hold on, I wasn't at all sure of his welcome," Hayley said, a touch sharply. "He left my eleven-year-old mom with a foster family and took off on his own. She didn't hear from him for years. She thought he'd abandoned her. And you heard him at the Cherry Pit. He said he had no sister at first."

Blake's outrage wavered. Okay, there were two sides to every story.

"I didn't know what kind of man my uncle is," Hayley went on. "That was the whole point of the client story. I needed time to find out what he was like, whether he would be open to being reunited with my mom."

"Why wouldn't he?" Blake said. "She's his sister."

"That's a good question and I would like an answer to it," Hayley said. "I'd like to know why it took him twelve years after he left home to even write to my mother. And why, when she wrote back to him, that was the end of communication. He never replied to her again."

"That doesn't sound like Gordon," Blake said. Loyalty kept him from saying what he was thinking, that if *he* knew he had a long-lost sister, he would have tracked her down if it took him his whole life. At least this explained all the questions Hayley had asked about Gordon and why she'd made excuses to spend time with him and talk to him.

"I couldn't blurt out the truth to my uncle right away and risk my mom being hurt from a knee-jerk reaction," she went on. "I didn't tell her what I was doing here at first either. If Gordon rejected her, then it would be better if she never found out. Better she kept her happy memories of when they were kids."

Okay, Blake accepted that. But it still didn't excuse Hayley's behavior. Dragging him around log houses all week, houses she had no intention of recommending to her fictitious client. "You could have talked to me. I would have told you what kind of a man Gordon was. I could have sounded him out for you. I could have acted as an intermediary."

"I almost did, a dozen times," she said. "I wanted to. But, I didn't know you either. You were so suspicious of me. You thought I was working for your enemy. I was afraid to confide in you."

And yet she'd confided other personal details, about her love life or lack of it, her brother. Unless all that was just chitchat to keep him on her side. When he thought of all the things he'd told her about his deepest thoughts and confessions, he felt so exposed that he wanted to punch something.

"I thought you were keeping me away from Gordon on purpose," she went on. "I didn't know if I could trust you, or him."

Blake was silent. It all made sense. Miscommunication, misinterpretation, missteps along the way. But the facts were clear, she'd stayed in Sweetheart, not for him as he'd hoped, but for Gordon. And fair enough given what she was hoping to achieve, but he could not go through the agony of a one-sided relationship again. Thank god he hadn't told her how he felt about her. Once she sorted things out with her uncle, she would be gone.

He wasn't just angry with Hayley for fooling him, he was mad at himself for falling for her. When he didn't refute her statement about being able to trust him, she turned pale, as if finally understanding just how deep the chasm was between them.

"You're still angry with me," she said.

"I wish you all the best," he replied, and a flicker of hope appeared in her eyes. "I don't think you're a bad person," he went on. "You're just not the woman I was hoping you were. You're not the woman I'm looking for."

The small ray of hope in her eyes died away, replaced by sadness and resignation. She rose and gathered her gloves and beanie from the side table. "I'll see myself out."

Blake sat where he was, mired in righteous anger and abject misery.

The sound of the door shutting made him start. He might not be able to trust her but that didn't stop him from liking her. And while he couldn't forgive and forget instantly, neither could he let Hayley go away unhappy.

He went outside onto the porch, shivering from the icy cold on the soles of his sock feet. "Where are you going?"

She had one hand on the door handle of her car. "To see Gordon. Did he say anything to you about the card, any hint that he knew who it was from? I told him he could call me, but I haven't heard anything."

"He didn't say anything about it," Blake said. "When he left the office, he hadn't opened it. It was mixed in with his papers. I'm not sure he even knows he has it."

Whatever color was left in Hayley's face drained away.

"Great. Still at square one."

"I'll come with you," Blake said, surprising himself.

"You don't have to," Hayley said.

"I want to," he said. "Family is everything to Gordon. He's got a lot on his mind right now, but everything I know about him tells me he would want to reconcile with his sister." And despite the crushing disappointment of Hayley lying to him, despite the fact that their romance was over before it had blossomed, she'd risked a lot and he wanted her to succeed. "Hang on, I'm getting my jacket."

She had the car running when he came out a few minutes later. "Thank you," she said quietly.

"I'll distract Brianna and Anita so you can be alone with Gordon while he opens the card," Blake said. He would help her in this one thing, and that would be the end of their friendship, or whatever it was.

As if she'd read his mind, she said, "I guess we won't be going skiing."

He didn't say anything; he didn't need to. But it was too bad. He'd been looking forward to spending time with her outside of work, to having fun with her doing an activity he loved. "You're under no obligation to do anything else on the spec home."

"I want to," she said. "For my uncle."

"Of course." Everything she'd done had been for her uncle. And why not? She didn't owe him, Blake, anything. Aside from a couple of meaningful looks, she'd never actually given him any reason to expect more.

"Sooner it's done, the sooner..." she went on before trailing away.

The sooner she could leave town. Right from the beginning, it was a given that she was always going to leave. Her home was in California and she had a thriving business there. Her mother and brother lived there. She might have fallen temporarily in love with Sweetheart. She might even have fallen a little in love with him, but that, too, was only temporary until she got back to her real life. The sooner he accepted it, the better.

"I'll be along in the morning, too, in case you need anything." He felt as if he was speaking now to a complete stranger instead of the woman he'd opened his heart up to and admitted things he'd never told anyone before, not even Carrie. How could he have felt so connected to her after such a short time and now have the bond they'd built over the week dissolve as if it had never been? And yet, that's exactly what had happened. Deceit had a corrosive effect on a relationship. More than that, it had made him distrust his own judgment.

"That would be good." Stopping at the corner, she reached out a hand to him. "Blake, I—"

He shook his head and looked straight ahead. "Keep going. Before I change my mind."

Chapter Thirteen

Friday evening, December 20, cont.

HAYLEY CONCENTRATED ON driving carefully on the icy road. The need to stay alert gave her something else to think about besides Blake sitting next to her like a brooding statue, silent and unforgiving.

She'd finally met a man she could foresee a future with, and she'd blown it. But looking back over the week, she didn't see what else she could have done. She'd had to trust her gut and make decisions on the fly as the situation evolved. If Blake hadn't been so suspicious of her at first, she might have trusted him enough to take him into her confidence. Even then, it wasn't certain. She hadn't known him, or Gordon and his family. Her mission on her mom's behalf had been her priority.

Gordon's lakefront home on the outskirts of town was of the same era as the Starr home, plainer than modern homes, but no less substantial. Landscaped grounds and a four-car garage contributed to a feeling of prosperity tempered by hominess. The wide-peaked roof and large picture windows glowed with rows of white Christmas lights, and a welcoming wreath of pine cones and holly trimmed the big front door.

Hayley parked in the driveway, and she and Blake walked up the cleared path. She glanced at her watch. Seven thirty-five. Hopefully, they would be finished with dinner. She pressed the doorbell.

"Good luck," Blake murmured.

"Thanks." She couldn't look at him, afraid she would start crying if she did. Losing him was the price she was paying for her mom's happiness, without any guarantee that the sacrifice would be worth it.

Anita answered the door, surprise and pleasure showing on her face as she glanced from Blake to Hayley. "Goodness, what brings you two out on such a wintry night? Come in. There's a fire going in the living room. We just finished dinner, but there's plenty left if you're hungry."

"No, but thank you," Hayley said. "I'm sorry to disturb you unannounced. Is Gordon home? I'd like to speak to him if I may."

"Certainly." Anita showed them into the foyer where she took their coats. "A glass of wine, cup of coffee?"

"Coffee would be great," Blake said. "I'll give you a hand."

"Gordon's through there," Anita said to Hayley, and opened the glass doors into the living room. "Go on in."

Hayley watched Blake and Anita disappear down a corridor to the back of the house and then walked into the other room. Her uncle was seated in a large leather armchair next to the fire, with a folded newspaper and a pencil. As she got closer, she saw he was concentrating intently on a puzzle of some kind. Sudoku.

"I like sudoku too," she said. "Is that a hard one?"

"Hayley." He set the paper and pencil on a side table and half rose. "Please, sit down. I didn't hear the door. Did Anita let you in?"

"Yes." She took a seat on the armchair opposite. "Blake's here too. I…" She trailed away, intimidated by the blank incomprehension in his expression. He had no idea why she was here. "Have you opened the card I gave you this morning?"

"What? No, it must still be in my briefcase. We had dinner as soon as I got home," he said. "I could get it."

"Please." Hayley's fingers tangled in a tight ball in her lap.

Gordon went out of the room, returning a moment later. Resuming his seat, he tore open the flap. He looked at the picture on the front of the card for several very long seconds, clearly trying to make up for his previous lack of interest by appreciating the snowy scene and the log cabin. "Very pretty. Thank you, Hayley."

"There's more," she said, willing him to move faster.

He opened the card, and her mom's handwritten, folded letter fell out. Gordon glanced up in surprise. "Is this from you?"

Hayley shook her head, too overcome to speak. "My mom."

He glanced at the signature on the card and stilled. In the tense silence, the slow ticking of the mantelpiece clock sounded overloud. Gordon's hands trembled. "Joyce. My sister."

She nodded. Tears seeped beneath her lashes. "I'm sorry I didn't tell you right away. I...I didn't know how. It's complicated."

His rimless glasses clouded, and he pulled them off, rubbing at his eyes. Then he looked at her at last, really looked. His sorrowful expression eased slowly into a smile that spread across his lined face, crinkling his weepy eyes. "Are you...her daughter?"

She nodded, her breath held.

"Come here." He rose, and she stumbled to her feet to embrace him. He hugged tightly, his wool cardigan rasping her cheek. Easing back, he held her at arm's length. His glasses sat askew, and his gray hair was mussed, but he beamed at her. "Why didn't you say something earlier?" he asked, touching her cheek in a kind of awe. "My niece."

"I didn't know if you would be receptive to meeting me," she said.

"Of course I am." He hugged her again. "You're my sister's child. And you have a big brother. What's his name again? No, don't tell me...Brad."

"Yes." Hayley dabbed at her eyes. "He's in the Philippines right now."

"I remember," Gordon said. "He's working for Doctors Without Borders. A very important job, that."

"Mom sent a photo of you and her when you were young." She handed him the still folded letter.

Gordon unfolded the paper and gazed at the images of himself at eighteen and Joyce at eleven years old. "I remember when this was taken." His voice caught. "We'd gone to the mall and just fooled around. I bought her ice cream." And then his face crumpled, and he covered his face, his shoulders heaving. "Oh, Joyce. Forty-seven years, wasted."

Hayley sat on the arm of his chair and put her arm around his shoulders, feeling his pain. She plucked a tissue from the box on the side table and handed it to him. "What happened? How did you lose touch?"

Gordon dabbed at his eyes. "After I finished high school I was champing at the bit to leave home. I'd been planning on going away for my whole senior year, but I didn't tell Joyce until the morning I left. I didn't want to upset her."

"The shock of your unexpected departure probably upset her the most," Hayley said.

"I realize that now," Gordon said. "She was wild, inconsolable. And angry! She tore me a new one. I felt terrible. But there was no future for me in that little town. I couldn't have taken her with me. She was just a kid, going to school. I had to harden my heart and walk away, leaving her crying and raging, even though it was the hardest thing I've ever done."

"She missed you," Hayley said. "She's always missed you."

Gordon nodded sadly. "I moved around a lot, wherever I could get work. I wasn't great at communicating. I sent the odd postcard but never put a return address because I didn't know how long I was going to be there. It wasn't a deliberate slight; I was just thoughtless, only thinking about what I was doing. But I never forgot her."

"You did write her a letter eventually, with a return address," Hayley said. "And she wrote back to you, although many months later. Then she never heard from you again. She thought you'd given up on her."

Gordon frowned, as if trying to piece together his memories of the time. "I wrote to her after I married Anita and we settled in Sweetheart. But I never heard back from your mom. A year and a half passed, and I wrote another letter. Again, no reply. I figured then that she'd disowned me as her brother. I was sick with regret, but part of me was also angry. She'd made me feel like a real heel for leaving her and then to not reply to my letter? No matter what, I was still her brother."

"Wait a minute, you didn't get her letter?" Hayley said. "That's strange. She definitely wrote to you."

"When?" Gordon asked.

"About ten months after she got your letter."

Gordon stared at her. "And she never got my second letter?"

Hayley shook her head. "No."

Anita and Blake came in then, with coffee and cake. Gordon explained about the card and told Anita that Hayley was his niece. Hayley got up and hugged her aunt, and tears started all over again.

"Brianna's going to be mad she went out tonight," Anita said, still holding Hayley's hand. "So that explains why she called Gordon to tell him to open your card. He didn't get around to it. Did she know?"

"I didn't tell her," Hayley said. "I wanted to, many times, but I wanted to speak to Gordon first."

"I guessed," Blake said. "Brianna and I talked about it after Gordon left the office today." He turned to Hayley. "She tried to call you, too, but it went to voice mail."

"I tried to call her back later, but never connected," Hayley said. "I was going nuts waiting, hoping that Gordon was going to call me. When he didn't, I decided to just come over. I want to apologize to you and Gordon and Brianna, for pretending I was here for another purpose."

"Don't say another word," Anita said, holding up a hand. "It took a lot of guts to come out here without knowing if you'd be welcomed."

Gordon nodded in agreement. "I'm happy that you came in person, that we got to meet you."

"I am too," Hayley said. She still couldn't look at Blake. Her aunt and uncle had forgiven her, but he couldn't.

Maybe he never would.

"Tell us the details," Anita went on. "How did the card, and your visit, come about? I've been trying to get Gordon to look for Joyce again for years, but he stubbornly maintained that his sister didn't want contact."

Hayley explained what they knew of the correspondence and the missing letters. "Gordon didn't get my mom's letter in reply to the first one he sent. Mom had a lot to juggle back then—kids, work, home—so it was about ten months before she wrote back." She paused, trying to figure out the timing. "She said she wrote at Christmas, the year I turned one year old. I'm twenty-nine so it must have been 1990."

"Wasn't that the year a huge blizzard shut down the highway for a week?" Anita said. "It was a terrible storm. A train got derailed and some trucks ran off the highway and lost their loads. I remember the Christmas parcel from my sister never arrived. I'm pretty sure that was 1990."

"That could explain it," Gordon said. "It didn't occur to me to connect the two things, because the blizzard happened so long after I sent my letter."

"The hazards of snail mail," Anita said. "Those were the days before cell phones and internet. We take instant communication so much for granted now."

"All I knew was, I'd sent two letters and gotten no reply," Gordon said. "I assumed Joyce had cut me out of her life."

"I don't know what happened to your second letter, unless…" Hayley paused again. "We moved when I was about two years old, from Los Angeles to San Clemente. You must have sent it to the old address, and it didn't get forwarded." Hayley shook her head. "All this time Mom thought you'd decided not to stay in touch."

"And if Joyce is as risk-averse emotionally as Gordon, neither would be the first to make another move." Anita gently prodded her husband. "See where that gets you, Honey?"

"I had to talk Mom into writing the card," Hayley admitted. "She was afraid he wouldn't want to hear from her."

"Well, I'm very sorry she thought that," Gordon said. "It's a terrible shame." Then he brightened. "She should come here and spend Christmas with us. You, too, Hayley. It would be wonderful to have everyone here. It's too bad that Brad is away, but maybe next year."

"I would love that," Hayley said, smiling. "Mom will too."

"Call her," Anita urged Gordon.

Gordon nodded and, overwhelmed again, took his wife's hand.

Hayley got her phone out and hit her mom's speed dial. "Mom, I—Yes, I'm still here. Yes, it's going really well." She smiled at Gordon. "I've got someone here who would like to say hello."

She handed Gordon the phone. Hearing his tremulous, gruff voice sent tears spilling again, and she had to wipe her eyes with her sleeve. Sensing movement at the edge of the room, she glanced up to see Blake slipping quietly out of the room. She started to rise to follow him but Gordon asked her for confirmation about something and she sat back down. A moment later the front door closed.

Gordon and Anita hadn't noticed, so intent were they on the emotional phone call taking place. Hayley's heart wrenched painfully. Was Blake walking home? It was only a mile or two, but it was cold. Should she go after him? Her mind bounced between wondering what he was doing and the conversation between her mom and her uncle. Then she stopped herself. Blake had made it clear that he didn't want her around. She should concentrate on the joyous celebration happening in the room. This is what she'd come for, after all, even though her happiness was tinged with pain. She'd found her mom's long-lost brother but, in the process, had lost what might have been the love of her life.

She left an hour later, exhausted and emotionally drained, although mostly in a good way. The evening had culminated in a plan for Joyce to come to Sweetheart for Christmas. Rather than driving back to California, Hayley would stay in town and pick her mom up from the airport in Kalispell on the morning of Christmas eve. In the meantime, Hayley had been invited to move into the guest room at Gordon and Anita's house to spend time getting to know her new aunt and uncle and cousins.

What Hayley hadn't realized when she'd agreed to this— not that she would have said no anyway—was that Blake was always included in the family's Christmas festivities. Well, she would deal with that when it came around.

Before she went to bed, she tried calling Brad again. Again, she got voice mail. She pushed away her frustration and hurt and gave him the benefit of the doubt. If she'd learned anything from her mom and Gordon's experience, it was that life was too short to hold a grudge.

At the beep, she said, "Hey, Brad. Just checking in to see how you're doing. I love you, and I'm really proud of you. Call me when you can. Merry Christmas. Stay safe."

She hung up, but wasn't satisfied by the brief message. So she got out her laptop and wrote her brother a long email telling him all about her time in Montana and Gordon and his family. Then she reminisced about past Christmases and the fun they'd had. Finally, she wished him a merry Christmas, wherever he was. She told him how much she loved him and hoped to see him again soon. That she didn't want them to ever lose touch with each other, no matter what happened, or how long they were apart.

Chapter Fourteen

Saturday morning, December 21

T HE NEXT MORNING, Hayley rose early and ate breakfast quickly, so she could get up to the spec home to apply the finishing touches. While she waited for her car to warm up, she checked her phone for messages.

Late last night Brianna had sent an emoji-filled text message expressing her happiness at finding out they were cousins that made Hayley grin. Her mom had also messaged, another rambling babble of joy ending with details about her flight arrival.

Still no message from Brad. She frowned and bit her lip, praying the prolonged silence didn't mean something bad had happened to him.

Not a cloud marred the blue sky this morning as she drove north along Route 35. Sunlight sparkled on the snow blanketing the lake and trees. After a stop at the florist, her back seat was filled with fragrant flowers. This was her favorite part of staging, when she'd done the hard work and could wander through the beautiful home admiring her handiwork.

Despite her best efforts not to think of Blake, thoughts of him infiltrated her mind, and she had to keep pushing them away. Whatever they'd had was over. She'd admitted she'd made a mistake and apologized, but it was never going to be enough. If Blake couldn't forgive her for this small thing that she'd done with the best of intentions, then he wasn't the man she wanted to spend the rest of her life with. People made mistakes, and it was important to learn to forgive sometimes.

When she arrived at the spec home, Blake's truck was there. Shoot. Well, she had to get used to talking to him, since she would be spending time in Sweetheart. She'd deal with him professionally—brisk, polite, cheerful. Above all, she couldn't let him see how hurt she was.

"Good morning," she said, coming through the propped-open door carrying an armful of flowers. Her heart lurched at seeing him, his dark hair tousled and sleeves rolled up over muscled forearms flexed from carrying disassembled pieces of slatted white furniture up the staircase.

He nodded a greeting. "I'm going to set this up in the small bedroom."

"Wonderful," she said, a little too exuberantly, not even asking what it was. "I'm here to do the flowers."

Obviously. Cue awkward silence. After a brief pause, Blake nodded and continued upstairs.

Hayley carried the flowers to the laundry room sink and

filled it with water. Then she went back to her car for the vases. On second thought, maybe only *she* had felt awkward. Blake's demeanor was totally neutral, as though she didn't affect him one way or another.

When she was done with the flowers, she headed up to see what Blake was putting in the small room. He had the sides of a vintage crib attached to the headboard and was about to screw on the end.

"Anita lent us this," he said. "It belonged to her kids."

"It's perfect." Her fingers traced the outline of a decal of a fluffy yellow duck. "Need any help?"

"Sure." He positioned the end board and one of the slatted sides together then pulled a screwdriver out of his tool belt. "Hold these pieces steady while I screw them together."

Hayley held the boards together. In an alternate universe, they might have done this for their own child. She listened to the sound of Blake's breathing, the faint rustle of his clothes, the squeak of the screw going into the wood. His strong fingers moved capably, handling tools with the ease of experience. Intelligence and strength, humor and purpose, generosity and loyalty. He really was the whole package. She wished fervently she could win back his trust, show him that she wasn't like Carrie. She needed him to smile at her again like she needed to breathe.

"Where do you want to put it?" he asked.

"In that corner, next to the window." She helped him carry it over. "I'll make another trip to the Antiques Barn. I saw the cutest mobile of old airplanes and some other vintage toys in a children's shop."

"A rocking chair would look good in here," Blake said. "I've got the one my mom used when she nursed me as a baby. I'll bring it over."

"That would be great," Hayley said. They both stood back and surveyed the room. In a flood of déjà vu, she felt as she had at his house on the point, as if they were planning their future home.

As if Blake, too, remembered that day, he abruptly turned to go.

"Blake?" she said softly.

He paused in the doorway but didn't turn around.

Her throat closed up and it was an effort to speak. "I just want to say, I'm sorry."

"You already said that," he said, impassively. "I got the message."

"But you're still angry."

Silence.

Finally, he said, still in that chillingly neutral tone, "Mostly at myself."

"I hope someday you'll forgive me. Now that Gordon and Mom are going to reconcile, this won't be my last visit. You work for my uncle, you're friends of the family." Her voice cracked. "I can't bear seeing you and having you be angry and, and…" *Don't hate me.*

"I've already let it go." He turned around. His eyes were

flat, the very lack of expression betraying the effort he was making to hide his feelings. "I'm sorry I said hurtful things yesterday. But you shouldn't feel badly about us. My prospects aren't great. Gordon got an offer from John Coates that he can't refuse. He hasn't said so yet, but I know he's going to sell. I won't work for Coates, so I'll probably be out of a job soon."

"I don't care what your job prospects are," she said with a dismissive shake of her head. "But don't you dare give up on yourself. The business is as much yours now as it is Gordon's. Buy him out."

"I would have to sell the house on the Point."

"Oh, no, you can't do that." Hayley subsided, seeing his dilemma.

"It might be enough," he mused to himself as if she hadn't spoken. "If I can work out a deal with Gordon that would protect his assets for his children."

Hayley was about to ask what he meant when Brianna called her name from downstairs.

"Hayley! Cousin!" Brianna yelled. "Where are you?"

Hayley laughed. "Up here," she called back.

Blake took the opportunity to leave the room. Hayley followed along the gallery. Brianna flew past Blake and pounded up the stairs, the large tote bag over her shoulder banging against her side.

"I knew we had to be related," Brianna said, throwing herself into Hayley's arms. Her latest Christmas sweater had giant pink snowflakes on a red background. "This is so exciting!"

Hayley hugged her. "I'm sorry I didn't tell you sooner."

"Oh, who cares," Brianna said. "It would have been hard to pop up into town and say to a complete stranger, 'Hey, there, I'm your long-lost niece.'" She began to unload the contents of her tote. "Look at what Angus and I just picked up at Antiques Barn. A bunch of vintage toys for the nursery."

Hayley's eyes widened at seeing the airplane mobile. "You must have been reading my mind. Come and see what Blake just brought around."

"Our old crib. I know. My mother mentioned she'd sent it over," Brianna confessed. "But let's go with mind reading. *Cuz.*"

Hayley grinned. If only Blake could have as uncomplicated a reaction to her as Brianna.

AFTER LEAVING THE spec home, Blake drove back to Sweetheart and dropped the rental skis off at Garrett's store. Putting the crib together had been child's play, but pretending not to care about Hayley was exhausting. He'd thought he didn't know how he felt about her, but seeing her this morning, imagining her and him together, had crystallized his feelings. Despite everything, he was in love. And love hurt. It would be almost a relief to be able to draw a line under this crazy interlude. He just had to get through Christmas, and then Hayley would return to California, and he could crawl back into his cave. He didn't even want to think about how Brianna would interpret *that*.

He found Garrett at the desk, checking inventory. "Hey, bro, just dropping these off."

"Put them over by the door to the back room," Garrett said. "How did it go? Did she enjoy the skiing?"

"We didn't go," Blake said. "Been busy staging the spec home."

"So, keep them and go tomorrow," Garrett said.

Blake carried the skis to the entrance to the back room. "That won't be happening."

Hearing the finality in Blake's voice, Garrett stopped what he was doing and really looked at him. "What's wrong?"

"Nothing, except...she's not the person I thought she was."

"Why not?" Garrett persisted. "You were so pumped about her."

"I'd rather not talk about it," Blake said.

"Oh, no, you don't. I know how that works," Garrett said. "You clam up and hide under a rock for six months or a year, suffering in silence. You're not leaving the store until you tell me what's going on."

"How are you going to stop me?" Blake put up his fists

in a mock fighting stance.

"Come on, man," Garrett said, not taking the bait. "What did she do?"

Blake dropped his arms. "She told everyone she was here to scout out a log home for a client. I spent days with her on this—"

"Yeah, I could tell you hated every minute of it," Garrett interrupted.

"And then it turns out there is no client, and she's not going to buy a house," Blake said. "Hayley is Gordon's niece. Her mom lost touch with him decades ago. Hayley was using me to get to him. Hanging around, checking *him* out before she revealed who she was."

"Wait, so you're jealous of your sixty-five-year-old boss?" Garrett said. "Dude, get a grip."

"Don't you get it? She lied to me," Blake said. "I spend a lot of time showing her around houses, getting her information and talking to her about log homes. It's not like I don't have enough to do without pandering to phony clients. She used me."

"Oh, I see," Garrett said as if he suddenly understood. "Like Carrie lied to you and used you."

Blake hesitated, then stuck to his guns. "That's right."

"No, that's *wrong*," Garrett said. "I hate to break it to you, pal, but it's not the same thing at all. Carrie led you on for over a year, letting you believe she was going to marry you when she had no intention of doing so whatsoever. Then she ran off and dumped you by text message. The woman was a complete b—"

"You don't need to say it." Blake frowned. "Okay, maybe Hayley's not quite in the same category."

Hearing Garrett outline the facts in stark terms, Blake had to admit the two women weren't comparable. Carrie had deliberately told him multiple lies and used him for her own personal gain, stringing him along for nearly two years without a qualm. Hayley had been keeping a secret for the sake of her mom and misled him, reluctantly, for a week.

He'd built it up in his head that Carrie and Hayley's actions were morally equivalent. Contrary to what he'd thought, he must not be fully over the hurt his ex-fiancée had inflicted if it could flare up over a misdemeanor. But recognizing the truth and convincing a badly bruised heart to trust again were two different things. Somehow, he had to let it go of the pain or he'd never be able to move on.

"Hayley came in here the other day to buy things for your skiing trip," Garrett was saying. "She's into you, man. Blushing every time your name was mentioned. Too cute. And she paid for her ski rental and told me to credit your account. Whatever you think she's using you for it's not free rental skis. Can't you talk to her, work things out?"

"I was too harsh on her," Blake admitted. "I need to apologize." Again. Then he remembered his work situation and confided, "Keep this under your hat, because it's not a done deal yet, but Gordon is likely going to sell Sweetheart

Log Homes to Coates Construction. I'll be out of a job and so will half our workforce."

"So you're afraid Hayley won't want you because you'll be unemployed," Garrett deduced.

"No," Blake began. She'd said she didn't care about his prospects but *he* cared. "I want us to be on an equal footing. I can't go to her with nothing to offer."

"You have solid experience and an impressive resume," Garrett said, reasonably. "You'll have a new job in no time. Anyway, how do you know what she'll say until you ask her?"

"Ask her what?" Blake demanded. "Will you stick around until I get back on my feet again? Why would she do that?" And that was the crux of it; the fear that Hayley wouldn't stand by him through a rough period. Carrie hadn't even stayed when he was on top of his game.

"Love will make people do crazy things," Garrett said.

"Like you'd know," Blake ribbed his friend. "You don't stay with anyone long enough to fall in love. Anyway, I've only known Hayley a week."

"Sometimes it takes months to fall in love," Garrett said. "Sometimes you crash into it." He cocked a finger at Blake. "Like you, my friend."

Blake said nothing. It was true. And it scared him to death.

"What are you going to do about it?" Garrett asked, clearly aware he'd struck a chord.

Blake didn't answer because he was too busy thinking. If he wanted to impress Hayley, then he couldn't sit around whining because he was going to lose his job. He had to fight back. He might not win against John Coates, but he had to try. Gordon wasn't some mercenary boss who only thought about the bottom line. If he could convince Gordon to hang on until he could buy him out over time, then they could keep all their employees, and everyone would have a good Christmas. And maybe he could convince Hayley to give him another chance.

"I've got to go. Catch you later," he said to Garrett. "I have another stop to make before everyone shuts up shop for the night."

Blake headed down the street to Starr Realty. Selling his house on the Point would break his heart, but it was the only way he could raise the money and convince Gordon he was serious about taking over the company. And the only way to prove himself worthy of Hayley.

STILL AT THE spec home, Hayley was gathering up the paper from the flower arrangements into a garbage bag. The Realtors would be here shortly to prepare for the open house, and she wanted to get out before they arrived.

Gordon poked his head in the doorway. "How is it going?"

"Hi, Uncle Gordon," Hayley said. "We're all ready to go."

He went into the living room and gazed around, lightly touching the replica of a Remington cowboy on a side table. "You've done an amazing job. Congratulations. And thank you."

"It was my pleasure," she said, smiling. "I don't often do the staging anymore, but it was really fun to decorate a log home. I hope I get a chance to do more."

"If you ever want a job, I'd put you on the payroll in a heartbeat," Gordon said.

Hayley tilted her head. "I thought you were planning to sell the business."

"I'm still thinking about it," Gordon admitted. "My children aren't interested, so what am I continuing for?"

"Blake," Hayley said. "He would buy you out if he could."

"He's always been like a son to me," Gordon said. "I wish I could give him the company, but I can't shortchange my own children on their inheritance."

"Couldn't you sell it to him over time, be like a silent partner, and still have part ownership in the company to pass on to your kids?" she asked.

"Coates is offering a huge amount," Gordon said. "I have to do what's right by my family."

"No matter what the human cost?" Hayley said.

"I'm not happy about his conditions," Gordon said. "But

it's a lot of money to turn down. And now I have a niece and a nephew I didn't know about."

Hayley held up her hands. "Oh, no. I don't want a thing from you, and I know Brad wouldn't, either. Mom's happiness is all I came for."

Gordon's frown eased into a smile at the mention of Joyce. "I can't tell you how much I'm looking forward to seeing her. It's too bad your brother can't be here. We're planning to have the whole family around on Christmas eve. Blake too."

Her smile faltered. "Wonderful."

"Is everything okay between you and him?" Gordon asked. "He seemed a bit funny this morning when I mentioned your name."

Hayley looked down at her hands. "He's mad at me because I wasn't truthful about why I came here."

Her uncle squeezed her shoulder. "That shows he cares. If he didn't, a little fib wouldn't bother him."

She gave him a rueful smile. "It's a little more serious than that."

"He'll come around," Gordon said. "Your heart was in the right place. He knows that. He's a good man."

"I know he is," Hayley said. That's why she'd fallen for him. A tiny flare of hope rose inside her. Was her uncle right? Could she convince Blake to give her a second chance?

Chapter Fifteen

Tuesday, December 24, Christmas Eve

"HEY, GORDON. GOT a minute?" Blake knocked on his boss's office door and hovered in the doorway.

"Come on in," Gordon put down his pen and leaned back in his chair. "Take a seat."

Blake dropped into a guest chair. "Big day, huh? Your sister arriving."

"That's right." Gordon passed a hand over his newly barbered hair. "Just hope she'll recognize me."

"She would never forget what her brother looks like," Blake said. "Is Hayley going to bring her here?"

"No, she'll take her to the house. I'm going home early, right after my meeting with John Coates. He'll be here any minute to get my answer to his offer."

"I know." Blake pressed his damp palms against his jeans. "That's what I wanted to talk to you about."

"I have something to say to you too."

Blake's insides turned over. He could just imagine. *You've been a great employee, I appreciate all you've done over the years, etcetera, etcetera, but I need to do what's best for myself and my family.* And he wouldn't blame Gordon for one second for taking Coates's offer. But he couldn't listen to that until he'd at least made his pitch. For the first time ever he didn't defer to his boss. "I'll be quick then."

Gordon glanced at his watch. "You do that."

"Okay." Blake drew in a deep breath. "I am asking you not to sell to Coates. Setting aside all the reasons why it would be bad for our employees and the town, and how he would destroy the reputation for quality log homes that you've spent decades building, I'm asking purely for my own sake. But, I have a plan that will hopefully be acceptable to you and your family."

Gordon's eyebrows rose, but he nodded. "Go on."

Blake got to his feet, too full of pent-up energy to sit. "Only one person loves this company as much as you do, and that person is me. I hold shares as you know, I've been buying them steadily over the years, but I don't have enough for a majority ownership. Yet."

Gordon looked past Blake, out the window onto the parking lot. "If I'm not mistaken, the Lexus that just drove up belongs to John Coates."

Blake swore under his breath. He went to the office door and poked his head out. "Brianna," he called. "Stall off Coates until Gordon and I are done in here."

"Sure," she said. "What's up?"

"Tell you later." Blake shut the door and noted Gordon's

bemused expression at the liberty he'd just taken. "With your permission, sir."

"Granted." Gordon bowed his head in assent. "But let's not keep him waiting too long."

"Of course. Where was I? Oh, right." Blake rubbed his hands together. "I've put my house on the Point up for sale. All the proceeds will be pumped directly into shares in Sweetheart Log Homes. I'll cut myself back to a subsistence wage and receive the balance as additional shares in lieu. I can't match Coates's offer, but I guarantee you will see a greater return on your continuing investment over time. Plus you'll have the satisfaction of knowing that your legacy will live on in this town. And not one employee will lose their job."

He stopped speaking abruptly. Through the door he could hear the muffled voices of Brianna talking brightly and John Coates's impatient tones. Blake looked at Gordon. "Well?"

"Okay," Gordon said simply.

"I know it's a lot to ask," Blake went on, not really hearing the answer. "But I promise I will maintain—Sorry, what did you say?"

Gordon chuckled. "I said, yes. We can work out the details later, but you're not going to eat ramen noodles for dinner for the next ten years. I never wanted to sell to Coates anyway." He rose and came around the desk to put his hands on Blake's shoulders. "You've always been like a son to me."

His voice was thick with emotion. "I wouldn't feel right letting the company go out of the family."

"Thank you," Blake said and embraced him in a brief, fierce man hug. "I won't let you down."

"I have the utmost confidence in you." Gordon cast a glance at the door. "We'd better let Brianna off the hook and give Coates the bad news. But, before you head out, come around to the house tonight for dinner. It's Christmas eve. Hayley and her mom will be there."

"Thanks, Gordon, but I don't know. Hayley and I aren't exactly on good terms." Blake hung his head. "I was upset, disappointed, worried about my future. I took it out on her. I haven't had a chance to make peace with her and I don't want to bring tension into your home, especially at Christmas."

"Nonsense," Gordon said. "I'd be honored if I could help in bringing you two together. Come, and talk to her."

"If she'll listen." Blake winced. "I acted like a jerk."

"If I know Hayley, she'll listen," Gordon said. "She's a warm and loving person. I know she cares about you."

"I hope you're right," Blake said.

"If you're half as passionate about her as you are about log homes, you'll do just fine."

Blake had to smile at that. As much as he loved log homes, there was no comparison. Hayley won hands down.

"WHAT DO YOU think?" Hayley asked Joyce as she drove slowly through Sweetheart. "Isn't it the cutest town you ever saw?" Gordon had told her he wouldn't get back to the house until just before lunch, so she was showing her mom around.

"I love it," Joyce said. "Oh, there's a realty office. Let's have a look. Just for fun."

"Would you seriously consider living here?" Hayley put on her indicator and turned into a parking spot in front of Starr Realty.

"I don't know. I wouldn't want to move too far away from you and Brad." Joyce paused a beat. "Before we go in, give me an update on this fellow you told me about. What's happening with him?"

"Nothing." Hayley's mouth twisted. "It's not going to work out."

"That's too bad, honey," Joyce said. "But, well, I guess you do have your business to run."

"I could start over. There's potential here in Sweetheart. And I happen to know a certain log home company that's in need of staging services." Then she sighed. "But I wouldn't move here unless Blake wanted me to, and right now I'm not in his good books, to put it mildly."

"Let's have a look at what's available anyway," Joyce said. "Gordon said we'd always be welcome to stay with them, but I might like to spend the summer here, and I wouldn't want to wear out my welcome."

They got out of the car and checked out the house listings on display in the window.

"Here's a cute little two-bedroom going for a song," Joyce said. "I could buy it as a second home, or you could live there, and I could visit. Oh, but I forgot, you're not ready to settle down."

Hayley pretended she didn't see the twinkle in her mother's eye. "I might be flexible on that."

"My, then, you *have* changed," Joyce said. "I distinctly remember—"

"Oh, my god," Hayley interrupted. "Blake's house on the Point is for sale." Wide-eyed she turned to her mother. "He's doing it so he can buy Gordon's business, which means Gordon decided to sell." She hurried toward the entrance. "I've got to buy that house."

"Just like that?" Joyce said. "Have you looked around?"

"Mom, it happens to be the most beautiful house in the whole world, but that's not the point," Hayley said. "Blake designed it and built it. He loves that house so much. He doesn't want to sell. He's sacrificing it so Uncle Gordon's company doesn't get bought out by John Coates."

"Slow down," Joyce complained. "Who is John Coates?"

Hayley quickly explained the situation. "Just the fact that Blake's letting it go so cheaply means he's trying to make a fast sale because he needs the money."

"But, Hayley, how is you buying the house going to help Blake?" Joyce said, clearly confused. "He'll still lose the property."

"Oh." It was true; she hadn't thought this through, hadn't had time. All she knew was that she couldn't let a stranger buy that house. It might go out of Blake's hands forever. "Not necessarily," she said, slowly. "I'll save it for him until he can buy it back."

"You're really going out on a limb," her mother said. "For what?"

"For a chance at happiness?" Hayley said.

"Well, that's worth taking a risk for," Joyce replied.

Hayley pushed open the door. Inside, the realty office all was quiet. The receptionist had already left for the day. "Hello?" she called.

Robert Starr came out of his office at the back. "Can I help you? Oh, hello, Hayley. Nice to see you again."

Hayley introduced her mother and, after a bit of small talk, explained that she wanted to put in an offer on Blake's house. "For the full price. I'm not going to try to bargain."

Robert produced the appropriate forms for Hayley to sign and gave her a receipt for the deposit. "I'll let Blake know of your offer. Once he's accepted it, we can go ahead and complete the purchase."

"Please don't tell him who is making the offer until he accepts it," Hayley said. Just in case he didn't want to sell to *her*.

If he decided at some point in the future that he didn't want the house, well, she would still have her dream home.

In the meantime, maybe this would convince him that she cared about him for his own sake and hadn't just been using him to get to her uncle.

"NERVOUS?" HAYLEY ASKED her mother as they walked up the path to Gordon and Anita's front door. She had her arm tucked through Joyce's for moral support, and she could feel her mom trembling.

Joyce's blue eyes glittered with unshed tears as she nodded. "A little. Happy too." She stopped at the bottom of the steps. "I'm scared that I won't know what to say to him."

"You'll know," Hayley assured her. "He's excited to see you. They all are: Anita, Brianna, and the boys."

"What are their names again?" Joyce asked.

"Aiden and Daniel," Hayley said. "I met them on Sunday for the first time. Everyone is so nice; you don't have to worry about anything." She hugged her mom. "Are you ready?"

Joyce gripped her by both hands. "Hayley, in case I don't get a chance to say this once all the hoopla begins, thank you so much for finding my brother for me. I still can't believe that all these years went by and I didn't make the effort. That he didn't. It's a terrible shame, and I'm so mad at myself."

"Oh, Mom, I'm happy I could do this for you. Don't

beat yourself up," Hayley advised. "You're here now, and everything will be fine. It's been a good lesson for me not to be so hard on Brad."

"Have you heard from him?" Joyce asked.

"No," Hayley said. Clearly her heartfelt email hadn't made an impact on him. But she wasn't going to waste time on recriminations that would only drive a wedge further between them.

"I'm worried about him," Joyce confessed. "Last time I talked to him, he was heading off with a convey of supplies to a remote village that had been hit by landslides. That was days ago. I haven't seen or heard from him since."

"Maybe there's no internet or phone reception in the village," Hayley said, damping down her own fears to comfort her mother. "I'm sure he'll be all right. We'll hear from him when he's able to make contact."

"I'm sure you're right, sweetheart." Joyce laughed gaily. "Sweetheart. I'll never use that endearment again without thinking of this town!"

While they stood there talking, the front door opened. Gordon, a big smile on his face, opened his arms wide. "I've waited forty-seven years to see you, Joyce. Don't make me wait another forty."

"Gordie!" Tears spilled from Joyce's eyes. She hurried toward her brother and met him on the middle step in a rocking bear hug.

"No one's called me that since I saw you last," he said,

kissing her cheek and hugging her again.

"Can you believe how stupid we've been?" Joyce put a hand on his jaw and gazed into his eyes. "You look just the same."

"I'm sure I don't, but you do," he said. "I can still see that little girl in a ponytail." His face crumpled and a sob escaped. "I'm so sorry."

"I'm sorry too." Joyce pressed her face into his chest and breathed in a long breath. Then she drew back and smiled through her tears. "Let's not waste time blaming ourselves. We've got a lot to catch up on."

"We surely do." With one arm around his sister's shoulders, Gordon put a hand out to include Hayley. "Come inside before we all catch our death of cold."

Hayley dashed the moisture from her own eyes and joined her mom and uncle. They trooped inside to the living room where Anita, Brianna, Aiden, and Daniel stood in a semicircle, waiting to greet Joyce. Introductions were made amid copious tears and hugs. Soon Joyce and Hayley were settled in comfortable seats around the fireplace. The men brought in extra chairs. On the coffee table stood an ice bucket with a bottle of champagne chilling and bowls of snacks.

Colored lights were strung around the wide double door leading into the dining room where the table was set for dinner with the best china, crystal, silverware, and linen napkins. Candles waiting to be lit flanked a centerpiece of glossy, green holly with bright red berries, circled by pine cones.

Gordon tore the foil off the champagne bottle and started to twist out the cork. He paused. "Where's Blake? We can't make a toast without him."

"He was here at minute ago," Anita said, glancing around.

Hayley was suddenly aware that her heart was beating faster. She barely had a minute to prepare herself when Blake walked in, carrying a load of firewood. His gaze flicked to hers and flared briefly. Before Hayley could interpret the emotion, he glanced away again. Dropping the wood in the bin next to the fireplace, he walked over to her mom.

"You must be Joyce," he said, holding out a hand. "I'm Blake. Welcome to Montana."

Joyce ignored the proffered hand and gave him a hug. "It's lovely to meet you. I've heard all about you from Hayley."

Hayley winced. *Thanks, Mom.* To forestall any more revelations, she nodded at Gordon, who was still holding the champagne bottle. "I propose a toast to the reunited brother and sister."

Gordon popped the cork and began pouring out the bubbly. When everyone had a glass, Hayley raised hers. "To my uncle and my mom, may they never know a moment's doubt about their affection for each other ever again."

"Hear, hear," Anita said, and everyone cheered.

"To my dear sister, who I have missed every day we've been apart," Gordon said. "May our families become close and enjoy many happy times together from now on."

Hayley put her arm around her mother and they hugged, exchanging a heartfelt glance. She knew Joyce's happiness, like hers, was tinged with sadness that Brad wasn't there to share in the occasion.

"To the continuation of Sweetheart Log Homes as a family enterprise," Gordon added, raising his glass again. "And to Blake, who will lead the company to even greater success in the future as general manager, and someday, as owner."

This generated a chorus of ohs and exclamations of delight. Hayley beamed at Blake across the room, and this time he smiled back at her, their eyes meeting for a long moment that made her feel dizzier than the champagne.

"To Hayley's gorgeous new home in this adorable town," Joyce said, raising her glass again.

This drew blank stares and a sudden and complete silence.

"Oops!" Joyce covered her mouth. "Maybe I shouldn't have said anything."

"So that was you who put the offer in?" Blake said to Hayley, his face ashen.

She swallowed. Nodded.

"No." He started shaking his head. Set down his glass. "No. Oh, no."

"Blake, I…" Hayley felt the blood drain from her face. "I was going to explain." She looked around the room at all the expectant faces and quailed.

Blake grabbed her by the hand. "Come with me."

He led her down the hall to the family room, also decked out in extravagant Christmas decorations. There was a second, smaller Christmas tree aglow with twinkling lights. Red ribbons swooped from the center of the ceiling, where a sprig of mistletoe hung, to the corners of the room festooned with pine boughs. Nutcracker toy soldiers lined up on the top of the upright piano, and candles glowed on side tables.

They came to a halt in the middle of the room beneath the mistletoe, although judging by Blake's scowl, that wasn't why he'd brought her here.

"Why are you trying to buy my house?" he demanded.

"Because it's for sale?"

"No, it's not. I'm taking it off the market," Blake said. "I forgot to call Robert and tell him that."

"It's too late," Hayley said. "I've already put in an offer."

"I haven't accepted it," Blake said. "We'll build you another house if that's what you really want."

"You don't need to worry," she assured him. "I have no immediate plans to move to Sweetheart."

"Oh?" He seemed taken aback. "I thought you liked it here."

"I love it." *I love you.* She couldn't look at him. Instead she studied the whorls in the grain of the hardwood floor.

"I'm sure I'll visit Uncle Gordon, but, you know, with things between us not going so well, it would be hard."

"Hayley, I want to apologize again for those things I said to you. I overreacted and I'm sorry." Blake sounded miserable. "There's a huge difference between a white lie told to maintain someone's privacy and deceptive lies like my ex told me. I would hate for me to be the reason you don't want to come back to Sweetheart."

"Blake, you won't lose your house," she said. "I only wanted to take it off the market so that some stranger didn't buy it. I was trying to help you so you would have enough money to buy Uncle Gordon's business. When you're able, you can buy the house back, no matter how long it takes."

It took a few seconds for that to sink in. "You would do that for me?" he said, wonderingly.

"I would do pretty much anything for you," she said simply.

Blake took her hand in both of his. "I'm working out a deal with Gordon. He's going to retire and be a silent partner. My job is secure, and I'll be able to keep the house. In fact, things will be even better than before since I'll be managing the whole company."

"That's fantastic," she said. "I'm so happy it worked out for you." She couldn't tear her gaze away from him.

"I love you," he said, and then smiled ruefully. "I know that sounds crazy after only one week."

"If you're crazy, then so am I," she said with a tremulous

smile. "I…I love you too."

"Seriously?" He laughed, incredulous and joyful.

"Seriously." She laughed then, too, a release of pent-up emotion. "There was another reason I didn't tell you who I was. Once I started falling for you, I was afraid to admit I'd lied for fear it would affect your opinion of me. Of course, that only made things worse when the truth did come out."

"I understand why you did it," he said. "What you did for your mom and Gordon proves that you're a good person."

"Do you forgive me?"

"Nothing to forgive." He put his arms around her and drew her close, burying his nose in her hair and breathing deeply. Then he stilled. "So can I have my house back?"

"I guess." Hayley pressed her face against his chest and sighed. "It's too bad though. I was looking forward to living there."

"You still could."

She eased back to search his face. "What are you saying?"

"Would you consider moving to Sweetheart?" he asked.

"I'll have to think about it. This might take a while." She put a finger on her cheek and pretended to ponder.

"Take as long as you need," he said earnestly. "It's a big step and we only just met—"

She shushed him by pressing a finger to his lips. "I don't have to think. The answer is yes, I would relocate for you."

"It's also an opportunity to expand your business," he

went on.

"It's okay, you don't have to convince me. I'm already in," she said. "Mom wants to buy a small house here. I can live there until we're ready for the next step." Until she'd proved to him beyond a shadow of a doubt that she was trustworthy and would stay.

"I want marriage, kids, the whole nine yards," he said. "But there's no harm in taking it slowly."

"I want all that with you too," she said. "When we're ready. For now I'll have to travel for clients, at least until I build up a base here. But that won't be forever."

"No matter how far you go or how long you're away," he said. "I'll be here waiting for you."

"Oh, Blake." Joy welled up in her then, making it hard to say another word.

Blake cradled her face in his large hands and held her gaze. In his warm dark eyes, she could see the love and commitment he felt for her. He lowered his mouth to hers in a tender, lingering kiss. Her tears wet his cheeks, and they broke the kiss to hug each other tightly, rocking gently. Then he showered her with more kisses, on her nose and eyes and neck, until they were both laughing from sheer happiness. She leaned up to kiss him again. This time, his arms tightened around her, and he spoke her name with longing, his deep voice making her shiver with excitement.

A loud *ding dong* sounded overhead. The doorbell, wired to ring at the back of the house, broke them apart.

"Saved by the bell," Hayley murmured wryly and smoothed down her blouse.

"Who could that be?" Blake said. "The whole family is here."

And then she heard her mother shriek. Hayley ran to the door. Down the long hall, she could see a familiar, beloved figure in the foyer, one arm in a sling and the other around their mother. Through the open front door, she could see a taxi pulling away.

"Brad!" she yelled and ran toward him.

Christmas morning

DISCARDED WRAPPING AND opened presents lay strewn around the Christmas tree in Anita and Gordon's living room. Outside, snow was falling in thick, fluffy flakes. Inside, all was cozy. A fire blazed in the hearth, and the whole family was gathered, perched on furniture or sitting on the floor, relaxed now after the excitement and laughter that had accompanied the opening of presents. A pot of coffee and a pan of freshly baked cinnamon buns sat on the coffee table, and everyone helped themselves.

Hayley sat next to Blake on the sofa, their hands linked. Seated on her other side, Brad was relating the story of how he'd broken his arm. He'd fallen while trying to rescue a little boy from the second floor of a house after the typhoon had taken the roof off and several walls caved in.

"I thought you just took supplies off the plane and put them into trucks for other people to deliver," Joyce said. "What were you doing climbing into houses with no roofs?"

"We were short-staffed, so I volunteered to drive a supply truck to the village," Brad told her. "When we got there, it was a disaster. There was no one else to help these people."

"Was the boy all right?" Anita asked.

"Yes, luckily I broke his fall," Brad replied. "His parents were fine, too, just very shaken up. After I broke my arm, I was sent stateside on the first available plane."

"How did you know where to come?" Hayley asked.

"Mom left me a message with the address," Brad said. "As soon as I got to Los Angeles I got straight on another plane and came here."

"When I gave him the address, I didn't know about his arm. I sent it just in case. I never thought he would actually get here." Joyce beamed at her son. "But I'm so glad you did."

"We all are." Gordon looked around at his sister, her children, his wife, and his own children, and the man he considered a son. "I'm so lucky to have such a wonderful family."

"Here, here," Joyce said, raising her coffee cup. "To family."

Everyone agreed heartily and after that, the group broke into several smaller conversations. Blake got up to stoke the fire and add another log.

Brad turned to Hayley and squeezed her hand. "Sorry I didn't write back to you. I got your email just before I headed out to that village and didn't have time. But what you said about spending time together and appreciating each other kept me going when I was bouncing along that dirt road back to the city with an unset broken arm."

"I'm glad." She reached up and hugged him. "Glad you're safe and here with us."

"Your new guy seems okay," Brad said, nodding at Blake.

"He's..." She searched for words that could express the fullness in her heart at having found such a wonderful man. "He's the one I've been waiting for all my life."

"So you're really going to move to Sweetheart?" Brad asked. "Are you sure you can handle a little town in the mountains after living in a big city like San Diego?"

"It already feels like home," she said. "Not just because of Blake and Uncle Gordon, although they both contribute to that feeling. It's weird, but as soon as I got here, before I met anyone, I thought I could live here. The mountains, the lake, the sky, and the open spaces calls to something inside me." She gave a helpless shrug. "I can't explain it, but it's real."

"I'm happy for you," Brad said. "But I'll miss you."

"You'll have to visit often." She punched him in his good arm. "No excuses."

"Hey, don't." Brad tried to tickle her, but she squirmed

away.

"Stop!" she said, breathless. "Stop or I'll I cry uncle."

They both looked across at their uncle Gordon and laughed. Gordon's eyebrows shot up in a questioning expression, making him look a little like an owl, and they laughed some more. Gordon smiled indulgently and glanced at Joyce who returned his smile with affection. Hayley blinked and touched a fingertip to her eye. There was so much love floating around, it was making her a bit silly.

Sobering, Hayley said, "Seriously, Brad, let's not ever lose touch with each other."

"Not going to happen." He squeezed her hand. "I'll make more effort."

"Good." Hayley glanced up to see Blake heading down the hall with the firewood basket. "Excuse me, okay? I'll be back in a minute."

She caught up with Blake at the back door. "Wait for me. I'll give you a hand."

He set down the basket and pulled her into his arms. "I was hoping you'd come out with me. It's a good twelve hours since I've had a chance to kiss you."

"What are you waiting for?" she purred.

He didn't need to be told twice. He lowered his head to hers, and she put her arms around his neck. Hayley melted into his arms and gave herself up to a kiss full of joy and the promise of the future. It lasted so long that Hayley finally had to come up for air, but she kept her arms around his waist and laid her head on his chest.

"Happy?" Blake asked in a low, gruff voice, whose vibrations she could feel clear through to her heart.

"Completely." She leaned back to smile up at this beautiful man of hers. "I feel as if all my Christmases have come at once."

The End

If you enjoyed this book, please leave a review at your favorite online retailer! Even if it's just a sentence or two it makes all the difference.

Thanks for reading *Long Lost Christmas* by Joan Kilby!

Discover your next romance at TulePublishing.com.

TULE
PUBLISHING

More books by Joan Kilby

The Starr Brothers of Montana series

Book 1: *The Secret Son*

Book 2: *A Baby for Christmas*

Book 3: *The Bull Rider's Return*

If you enjoyed *Long Lost Christmas*, you'll love these other Tule Christmas books!

Royally Abandoned
by Sarah Fischer & Kelsey McKnight

The Christmas Contest
by Scarlet Wilson

A Texas Christmas Wish
by Alissa Callen

About the Author

Award-winning author Joan Kilby writes sweet, sexy contemporary romance with a touch of humor. When she's not working on a new book Joan can often be found at her local gym doing yoga, or being dragged around the neighborhood by her Jack "Rascal" terrier. Her hobbies are growing vegetables, cooking, traveling and reading—not necessarily in that order. Happily married with three children, Joan lives in Melbourne, Australia. She loves to hear from readers so feel free to drop her a line.

Thank you for reading

Long Lost Christmas

If you enjoyed this book, you can find more from all our great authors at TulePublishing.com, or from your favorite online retailer.

TULE
PUBLISHING

Made in the USA
Columbia, SC
15 November 2023

26376684R00162